AIR BOUND

AIR BOUND

DRAGON OF SHADOW AND AIR BOOK ONE

JESS MOUNTIFIELD

LMBPN Publishing
PMB 196, 2540 South Maryland Pkwy
Las Vegas, NV 89109

Version 1.11 June, 2021
eBook ISBN: 978-1-64971-691-0
Print ISBN: 978-1-64971-692-7

For everyone who ever really wished they were an elf. Or that they had a dragon.

— Jess

THE AIR BOUND TEAM

Thanks to the JIT Team:

Dave Hicks
Dorothy Lloyd
Zacc Pelter
Deb Mader
Veronica Stephan-Miller
Misty Roa
Diane L. Smith
John Ashmore
Rachel Beckford
Larry Omans
Kelly O'Donnell
Jackey Hankard-Brodie

If I've missed anyone, please let me know!

Editor
SkyHunter Editing Team

CHAPTER ONE

Block. No, not like that.

I sighed, watching my sensei spar with one of the newer students, who was in a heap on the floor. And a simple block would have saved them.

"Aella, you next," he said, his eyes boring right into me. No doubt he'd heard the sigh. At least I hadn't been saying my instructions out loud. That was an improvement on my usual lack of self-restraint.

I walked onto the mat and took a deep breath to help myself stay calm. That was my biggest problem. Keeping calm.

"Think you can do a little better?" Rick asked, bowing to me. I bowed back, not answering. My sensei often taunted me. A few times I'd wondered if he thought I was arrogant and needed knocking on my ass a time or two, or if he knew it would make me angry and lose my cool. I had no idea which.

Was my sensei a jerk or trying to help me grow? Who knew? But either way, he was the only sensei teaching at this time of day, so here I was, doing my best to keep cool while Mr I'm-going-to-try-and-flatten-you did just that.

No sooner had I brought my fists up to defend myself than Rick attacked. After two quick jabs to my torso he attempted a roundhouse kick. I dodged the first two and blocked the kick, bouncing back on the balls of my feet to get some distance and look for an opening of my own.

But Rick kept coming, moving forward in little steps, each fist aiming for my torso as it came darting out. I was stuck in response mode, dodging, blocking, and creeping backward.

"Not in the mood to spar?" Rick asked as I retreated so much my back foot slipped off the mat and onto the floor. Instantly, both of us stopped our elaborate dance and moved back to the center of the mat. Had our match been a tournament I'd have lost a point, but Rick wasn't scoring us. This was just so he could show off. Or teach. Again, I wasn't sure which. Maybe both.

Focus. You've got to land something before the end of the class.

Narrowing my eyes, I concentrated, bowed with him rather than after, and launched straight into an attack of my own. Throwing my back fist forward, I twisted my body to give it more reach. Rick blocked, a light appearing in his eyes as he tried to counter.

I'd expected that and blocked as well. Continuing to bring my body around in a circle, I leaned away from him, lifted my back leg, and thrust for his stomach. My reactions were slow, however, and he caught my foot.

Spinning it, he used my momentum to push me even further. It knocked me off balance, and a sweep of his leg took my other foot out from underneath me. I landed on my front with an oof, my hands catching me in time to take some of the force out. My white-blonde hair covered my face, my ponytail unable to keep it all out of the way.

I flicked my head to get my hair out of my eyes and looked for my sensei. He was grinning, almost bouncing from one foot to the other as he waited for me to get back into the match.

I growled as I got to my feet, feeling the first rush of anger, but he danced backward, lighter on his feet than looked possible from his muscular frame.

For a moment I took my eyes off him, noticing over half the class was watching us, and by the time I looked back a fist was flying toward me. I managed to block it. Just. But I was so caught off-guard that the next punch tapped me right in the ribs. He pulled it at the last minute, making sure only my pride was wounded.

My head wasn't in the game. And Rick knew it.

He bowed, a smug grin on his face. If we hadn't been sparring, I'd have thumped him, hard. But there were rules, and I wanted to stay in this class. I couldn't find another that was compatible with my job.

As I thought about the waitressing I had to do next, I glanced at the clock on the right-hand wall. It said eight past seven.

Oh hell! I was late. The class was meant to finish at seven, and I still had to change, get to the bus stop, and ride to the small strip where the restaurant was. My shift started at seven thirty, and I usually walked out of the building with my uniform on.

I ran from the room, waving and calling bye over my

shoulder, but I didn't hold out much hope. One of the parents of a teenager in the group held the door open a fraction of a second before I hurried out.

The solid floor of the school corridor outside felt cold against my bare feet, but I ignored the sensation as I hurried for the changing rooms on the other side.

My bag was hanging up where I left it. I grabbed it and pulled out my uniform. Not giving a second thought to anyone else in the room as they took their time coming in, the class finished, I quickly took off my gi and the sweaty t-shirt I'd worn underneath it.

With no time to even consider a shower or doing more than spraying on some deodorant, I pulled my uniform on and stuffed everything else back in my bag. Only as I was heading back out of the changing room door did I realize I'd buried my purse and my bus fare along with it under-neath all my clothes.

Trying to root for it with one hand, I shuffled down the hall. I'd gone a few feet when Rick appeared, coming out of the gym along with the last stragglers.

"I'll need another month's payment on Thursday, Aella," he said, his eyes fixed on me.

"I know. I won't forget," I replied, hurrying on as if it wasn't important. In truth, it wasn't. I never forgot. And I'd only ever been late paying him once. But Rick had never seemed to like my resistance to setting up a direct payment. I gave him cash. At the beginning of every month.

As soon as I found my purse I stuffed it in my mouth and continued to shuffle as fast as I could while I used both hands to shove the loose clothing back in the bag and pull the drawstring to do it back up again.

Once the bag was slung over my shoulder I went to check the time on my phone. I patted my pockets, but it wasn't in them.

Shit!

I opened the bag yet again, and continued to shuffle on anyway. But by the time I reached the door out of the school and into the darkening LA city, I was sure it wasn't in the bag either.

I stopped and patted my pockets again, trying to think of when I'd had it last. It must have been while in the building. I could remember checking the time as I arrived. I'd been a few minutes early and enjoyed the hot shower for a bit. Mine was broken. Again.

Sighing, feeling the back of my neck and shoulders go tense, I turned and jogged back up to the changing rooms. I was halfway back when another of the women in the class appeared, holding my phone.

"Found it under a bench not too far from my shoes. Must have slipped off or something," she said as she put it straight into my outstretched hand.

"Thanks," I said, my gratitude genuine as she'd handed it over and didn't just keep it. Not that it was worth stealing. It wasn't the latest tech and was more than a little scratched.

She'd saved me time and effort though. As I flicked the screen on to check the time, I groaned. I was more than a little late.

All the time I'd made up changing so fast had already been lost. My only hope was for the bus to be late.

Jogging back again, I hurried for the door, still the first to leave, but not by much. The school opened out onto a long road full of apartment towers. There wasn't a lot else, but further up I could see a row of shops and a liquor store. At this time of night, only the small convenience and liquor stores were open, everything else shuttered up, graffiti covering every inch of metal and brick.

I hurried toward these, the bus stop just outside, but I was still a couple of hundred yards away when the bus came up in a rush of rumbles, squeaks, and hot air. It screeched to a halt, the brakes in need of some TLC, before spitting out people in dark clothes and hooded sweatshirts, with their headphones on and shoulders hunched as they hurried away toward the foreboding apartment blocks.

Shitsticks.

There was no way I was going to get there in time. Regardless, I picked up the pace, making the bag I carried bounce against me with every stride. Sometimes the driver would notice and wait on the few occasions I was late, but I knew I was still a long way away. At a hundred yards, give or take, the driver indicated and pulled off again.

I stopped instantly, already feeling exhausted. Having to run several hundred yards after a grueling karate lesson was less than fun. But without the bus to get me to the restaurant, I was going to have to.

Glancing at my phone again, I gritted my teeth and tried to find some more energy. I had nine minutes until my shift started. Nine minutes to get a mile and a half or so down the road. I could do it if I ran, probably. But already my legs were protesting and I had to slow. Not to mention the hunger gnawing at my insides.

There was always an emergency snack bar in the side pocket of my bag, alongside a water bottle. I'd already drunk most of the water during the lesson, but I grabbed the snack bar now and munched on it.

As I ate, I imagined the reaction I was going to get from my boss. I wasn't late often, but I knew even once a month for just a minute or two was something he would pick up on. I pictured his balding head now, the hair combed over and slicked with grease, and his chubby fingers that would point at me. The thought made my shoulders ache with tension.

I stuffed the last of the bar in my mouth in the most unladylike fashion and hurried along. The streets were still fairly busy, and more than once someone honked as they drove past, but in LA you got used to that kind of thing. Honks weren't too bad. You could ignore those. Sometimes I even shoved headphones in so I could pretend I hadn't heard them.

As long as no one catcalled or approached. It was just everyday LA.

On the way, I passed even more apartment blocks, some office buildings, and the occasional alleyway with dumpsters, pets, and its own distinct aroma of trash, drugs and urine.

This was one of the worst parts of the city. Here we were worlds away from the stars. The smell of weed was everywhere, the smell of piss anywhere it wasn't, and music blared from open windows.

Most of the time you could forget there were problems here, even with the sweet sickly smell of dope, but now and then you heard yelling, sirens, or even a gunshot. I tried not to think about what it all meant. I'd been here long enough that I'd seen most things. And I knew in this part of the city there were plenty of problems, but it was all I could afford, and I wasn't sure I was any better than the rest anyway.

As I passed yet another large block, about halfway to work, some younger men came out of one of the side doors, probably a fire exit, laughing and joking about something, passing a joint around and carrying a couple of six packs. There were five of them, and they talked loudly, boasting about someone called Shane getting one over on a Liam.

I slowed for a moment, letting them get ahead despite knowing it would lose me some time. They hadn't noticed me yet, and I preferred to keep it that way.

"Hey, Craig, come check this out. There's a cat down here without a tail," one of them said as they passed the next alley.

I gritted my teeth as they all slowed to a crawl and Craig moved a little closer to peer down. If I didn't get past them soon, I was going to be so late I'd get fired on the spot.

Trying to decide which trouble I wanted to handle that evening, I growled and clenched my fists. I needed the money. It was no good. I was going to have to pick the moment and hurry past.

Thankfully the cat seemed to be far more interesting than I was, and the men moved deeper into the alley and out of my way. I didn't jog, not wanting to draw attention to myself, but my heart hammered in my chest as I went past until I was on the other side of the alley.

"Here, kitty," one of the men said as I was just going out of sight. I didn't glance their way, but I doubted the cat was going to appreciate whatever they had planned for it. Boredom and not enough money or future left young men like them with some strange ideas of what fun should look like. It was enough to make me feel angry, but not enough to make me take on five men by myself.

I checked my phone again.

Oh, shitsticks. I was late, but as I turned the next corner I was on the home stretch. Down the road, a few blocks away, I could see the diner. Lights lit up the parking lot, and already it looked busy. That didn't bode well for me.

Again I picked up the pace, aware my breathing was already less than calm. I was great at short bursts of speed, sprinting and quick little jabs and uppercuts in a fight, but I wasn't as fit as I ought to be, and my legs weren't that long. At five foot four and a half I was on the shorter side of life.

But hope filled me as I reached my destination and I couldn't see the boss' car. Maybe he was sick or something and I'd only have one of the other waitresses to contend with.

It was my last-ditch hope as I sprinted the next couple of hundred yards. Not wanting to appear quite so desperate, I slowed past the hotel that sat just back from the road, this side of the restaurant.

The lights were on and the front door was open, but that was how it always looked on a Friday night. No doubt some of the people staying there were already in the diner. There was a deal between the two for the diner to provide breakfast and dinner as part of the hotel package. I'd be serving plenty of those customers tonight.

They were the hardest to look after, most of them tired, irritable, and wanting everything to be on their tables within seconds. And they were the worst tippers. They didn't get a bill, so some of them didn't even tip, but they expected the same service anyway.

As I was heading past the open door to the hotel a man came hurrying out, almost trotting down the steps. The face was slightly familiar. Despite that, he fell in beside me, flashing me a smile that was far too broad and lit up his eyes in a strange way. I blinked, sure for a second that they were yellow, but no sooner had I thought this than he turned forward and I couldn't get a good look anymore.

"You were the waitress from last night, right?" he asked, confirming the familiarity. Another hotel customer who was coming for dinner.

"Probably," I replied, still trying to calm my breathing and in no mood for conversation.

"Great. You working this evening?"

"I'm not wearing this uniform for the fun of it."

He glanced my way, but he didn't smile again and the look seemed odd. He wasn't checking me out either, but it was almost as if my uniform was suddenly fascinating to him and now he was studying every element of it one by one, filing it in some storage cabinet in his mind.

Thankfully, we arrived at our destination and I left him at the stand to be seated while I hurried through to stuff my bag somewhere and grab my apron. I'd made it. And less than ten minutes late. I'd survived another missed bus and hurried walk to work.

CHAPTER TWO

"Aella-Faye, you're late!" my boss called from behind me. I winced before grabbing the apron just underneath my hands and turning.

"Sorry, Mr Walker," I replied. "Bus driver was an asshat again today and wouldn't let me on without the right change. I walked as quickly as I could."

Mr Walker studied me for a moment, but I smiled as if I'd just told him I was willing to work another fifteen minutes at the end. I probably would. I often did to help get the place cleaned up, but I pretty much never got paid for it. No doubt it was one of the few things that had helped me keep the job. Scott Walker was not known for keeping his temper, and staff turnover was pretty high.

"You'd better get out there and take care of your tables. I've had Ginger seat some customers in your section, but no one has taken their orders yet." The boss nodded at me as if he'd told me off, but I smiled again and picked up my order pad and pen. You'd think in this day and age we'd be like a lot of the other diners and restaurants in LA and have fancy tablets and order systems, but we were in the cheap area and Scott Walker wasn't going to pay for anything more than the basic setup.

Sticking my pen behind my ear, the end tucked in my hair, all of it now in a neatened ponytail, I hurried back out to the restaurant floor.

There were always three of us on busy nights. Me, Ginger, and Khaleesi. Ginger shot me a glare as I hurried over to my first table, then she headed to the kitchens with a tray full of empty dishes and screwed-up dirty napkins.

Despite my first customer being the strange guy from the hotel, I plastered the usual smile on my face.

"So, what'll it be, sweetie?" I asked, blinking a few times to give my eyelashes a bit of a flutter and draw attention to my violet eyes. With any luck it would make his tip more generous. He might be a bit creepy, but I probably wouldn't see him again after today. He was an out of towner, and that meant I could afford to be a little more encouraging without it leading to long-term trouble. He ordered quickly, and thrust the menu into my hands so forcefully I fumbled. Reacting, I caught it before it could hit the ground.

Without another thought about it, I hurried to the next table and the next taking orders from the recent customers and clearing up dirty plates for those who'd arrived on the previous shift. Finally, I seated a bunch of forty-something men all dressed in suits, loose ties, and undone top buttons, making it obvious they were done with work for the day.

"Hey, gorgeous, get us all some beers. And put it on a tab, would ya? We've got the company paying tonight," the one nearest the edge of the booth asked as soon as they were seated and I'd finished handing out menus and reeling off the specials.

"Beers all round," I said. "And we'll sort the bill however you need at the end, sweetie."

I walked away, not giving them a chance to ask me anything else. I knew their type; they were going to take forever to decide and then make a dozen little requests for changes. I'd make sure my other customers all had everything they needed first. That way if they took a while, no one else would have to wait for me too long.

Mr Hotel-Dinner was the first to get his food, a rare steak and fries. I took it over, along with a tray of sauces, and placed it down with a flourish. He reached straight for one of the sauces and almost collided with my hand, throwing me off my usual rehearsed speech.

"You have hair naturally that color?" he asked while I recovered, not looking my way but putting the sauce back unopened and picking up his knife and fork as if he was going to start eating as it was.

"Yup, all natural and white-blonde," I replied, my brain still catching up. "Can I get you anything else?"

"With your ears, too, that must make you very special." He looked straight at me, not answering my question.

"I don't know, really. Haven't paid attention much to other people's ears. If you need anything else, just give me a wave and I'll come right back."

I walked away before the conversation could get any creepier. I knew I had striking features. And a pretty zany name, but here in LA all the waitresses did. I was in the city where everyone wanted to be an actor, or a dancer, or some kind of fashion designer. If you weren't born with some kind of special name and look, you created it and hoped it would get you noticed.

Where I grew up, I was strange and the odd one out. Here I was just like everyone else, even if I didn't have proper earlobes and the tops of my ears had a slight point to them. If I'd known who my parents were, I'd have asked them where I got it from. But I didn't.

I was adopted, and I hated being reminded of it.

Already feeling like my crappy day was getting even crappier, I brought a drink to a couple sitting a bit more out of the way. They were clearly trying to have a date, but it wasn't going very well, and then I only had my rowdy table of men to go back to.

They were on their second round of beers by the time the food arrived and I'd gotten it all on the table. As I suspected, they'd been fussy with their options. Thankfully the kitchen staff had gotten it all right, but they were already so distracted and buzzed that they got confused about whom the different meals were for. I had a good memory and soon had them sorted out, but I could feel myself struggling with the smile and the pitch to my voice.

I wanted nothing more than to growl, glare, and tell them to take a jump off a bridge.

"Can I get you anything else?" I asked, not wanting to at all.

"Actually, you could, gorgeous," Mr. In-charge said, looking straight at my chest instead of my face.

I made my smile grow a fraction, trying hard not to grimace by accident.

"Do you think I could get a quick peck on the cheek?

14

That lipstick of yours looks a mighty fine color. I'm sure it'll set off my skin the way it does yours."

I rolled my eyes, unable to stop myself, then sighed and walked away. It was never worth saying anything in response to that kind of question. Ignoring the behavior was a shitty way to deal with the problem, but it appeared it would be one of those nights.

I went straight to another table to take their order, giving him no chance to call me back just yet. Hopefully his colleagues would distract him before I was free again.

"Do you know what you'd like to order?" I asked the small family who'd arrived a few minutes earlier.

"Hmmm," the father said while the mother cooed over her baby, waving a rattle for it to try to grab. "What do you recommend?"

Shit on a stick, sawdust and hay, or the ashes from the fire pit, I thought but didn't say. I didn't care.

"How hungry are you?" I asked, never answering the recommendation question either. The mother seemed to notice me then and sped things along, ordering for herself and suggesting something he agreed with in a fraction of a second. I was quick to take the opportunity to leave, writing it down as I went, not wanting to give him the chance to change his mind. By now I was so tense I knew the smile was slipping.

As I went back past the businessmen, Mr Give-me-a-kiss was standing, either coming or going from the toilet, his fly half open. I ignored him, looking ahead, but as I went past, he reached out and grabbed an ass cheek. Without thinking, I whirled around, latched on to his wrist with my hand, and continued to turn.

With my momentum, I spun his arm up beside his back and then pushed his body forward until I'd slammed the top of his chest and his head into the table. The force rocked a beer over, spilling it all over a different suit. It also made Mr. In-charge yelp, but I cared less about that.

"I am *not* an object," I said, almost growling. *Great*, my head berated me. *That's really going to make him think you're all together.*

"Let me go, you crazy bitch," he replied, the rest of the table and no doubt most of the restaurant staring.

"Not until you apologize." I pushed his arm a little higher, making it clear I was in control.

"What is going on here?" Mr Walker yelled, coming closer as he did. I groaned before I glanced his way. His face was already red as he waddled toward our table.

"This man assaulted me," I said, still not letting him go, but Mr Walker wasn't looking at me. He was far more concerned about the customer. Sensing I wasn't going to get an apology, I let the man go and backed up. He straightened, trying to sort his jacket out, but the front was smeared with grease and various condiments. I'd flattened him into the remains of his own dinner.

"I'm so sorry, sir," Mr Walker said, helping Mr Suit remove his jacket. I stepped back, feeling both furious and worried all at the same time, until my stomach was a knot and my whole body was tense.

"Your waitress needs a muzzle or something. All I did was reach for her to get her attention and she freaked out," the creep said as Mr Walker assessed the damage to the jacket.

"You grabbed my ass," I yelled back.

"My office. Now," Mr Walker said. His hand locked on my arm, and he pulled me away. This time I held back my instincts to defend myself physically. I was in big trouble, but I had no intention of backing down. I'd had it with people treating me like crap.

On the way past several customers, I noticed they were all staring, some of them looking at me like I was mental, but the couple on their date were sadder, trying to smile at me as I caught their eyes. Had they witnessed it?

"Ginger," Mr Walker said in a loud sort of whisper. "Gentleman on table fifteen. Offer to dry-clean his suit and wipe his bill. Get them whatever they want."

Ginger looked at me and then Mr Walker, before nodding and hurrying off to do as she was asked. He didn't stop as we went through the staff door and into the small office where he handled the paperwork.

"You're fired," Mr Walker said as soon as the door was shut.

"But, Mr Walker, he sexually assaulted me. All I did was defend myself."

"I don't care what you think he did, Aella. Get your things and go. You've been warned before about your atti-tude, not to mention being late. I get women coming in here all the time asking to be waitresses. I'm done with your antics."

"But..." I trailed off as he opened the door again and stormed back out.

Taking several deep breaths, I tried to fight the tide of rising panic. What was I going to do? I couldn't be fired. I needed the money. I was barely surviving as it was.

A thousand thoughts came crashing down on me, and I

sank into the nearest chair. It stank of body odor and whiskey, but I didn't take it all in as tears began to flow down my face. I needed my job.

Not long after, the door opened again and the chef came in. He was a larger man, tall, but old enough and fond enough of his own cooking that what might have once been a well-built figure was now a little less so. He wrapped his arms around me.

"I'm sorry, chica," he said. "I know you probably felt in the right, but Scott's right. You can't assault the customers, even when they've gone for a feel."

"I know, but it's reflex. I've even trained half the waitresses that have come through here to do the same. We should be allowed to defend ourselves," I said, the tears stopping, but I still sounded higher-pitched than normal.

"Tell that to those who sue. Scott's the one who'll have to pay if they sue for it."

I let out a long exasperated sigh and sat back down again, wiping the wetness on my cheeks away with the handful of tissues the chef materialized from nowhere.

"I've managed to persuade him to pay you what you've earned and not take the dry-cleaning charge off, but you'd better go before he comes back and decides he's still mad."

Nodding, I got to my feet. I didn't trust myself to speak. Just thinking about it again made me furious. My fists clenched around the damp tissues before I strode out of the room and went to the small area the staff kept their belongings in. I stopped a moment, taking another deep breath before I pulled my jacket back on over my uniform and grabbed my bag.

Ginger appeared as I did and gave me a big hug as well.

I returned it. More out of politeness than anything else. Ginger and I weren't the best of friends. And I knew she wasn't truly that sorry to see me go.

"Won't be the same without you," she said, but despite the serious, concerned expression on her face as she spoke, her eyes lit up as she hurried back out to the restaurant area. She'd be getting all my tips that evening.

Mr Walker came back before I could follow, a small check in his hand. He took one look at me, and his angry expression softened.

"I know you need the money, so here's your wages. I've paid you for today."

"Thank you," I said, as I took the small pocket of cash. "But, please—"

He shook his head as he lifted his hand and cut me off.

"I know you regret what you did, Aella, but I can't put up with it any longer. You've been on your last warning for months. And then something else happens and I decide to forgive you. Enough is enough."

I sighed and opened my mouth to argue further, before I closed it again. There was no going back. Not this time.

"Goodbye," he said. "And good luck. I'll give you a reference when you need it. You worked hard, even if you have a temper."

I nodded, not agreeing with his assessment but willing to take the peace offering. I was going to need the reference. Waving goodbye to the rest of the staff, I grabbed my stuff and walked out of the restaurant.

Trying not to look around as I did, I noticed several of my customers had gone, no doubt giving Ginger a great tip instead of me, but I couldn't worry about that. I had some money to go home with at least.

Not sure what else to do, and feeling more tears flow, my feet carried me away, my head held high as I tried to fight my emotions. I'd had that job longer than all the other waitresses put together, and I was leaving it all because the wrong guy had come in and taken advantage at the wrong time.

I wanted to scream, and puke, and cry, and run away. I'd had enough.

And a part of me wanted to go back and give the customers a piece of my mind. Before I could, however, Mr Hotel-Dinner came out of the shadow beside the hotel, making me jump.

"Sorry about your job," he said. "I... uh... saw what happened."

"Thanks," I said, picking up the pace a little and trying not to look too bothered by his sudden presence. The bus stop was just beyond the hotel, so I headed that way, grateful I knew he'd be heading into the large building on the way past.

I tried to wipe the tears away, sniffing a little as I did.

"Oh, here," he said, pulling a handkerchief out of an inside pocket, but I shook my head and showed him the tissues I clutched in one hand still.

"No, don't get your nice handkerchief dirty on account of me," I replied. "I've got plenty of tissues." *And who carries those things anyway?* It was old fashioned. The kind of thing your grandpa did, or rich men in films.

Stuffing it away, he continued to walk beside me for a moment.

"Enjoy your stay," I said, motioning to the hotel entrance, which was still lit up and open, as he started to look like he'd come past it with me. He stopped, glanced at the hotel, not convincing me that he wasn't about to stick around, but then nodded.

With relief, I watched him head up the steps. Immediately, I made my way to the bus stop. It was nothing but a bench and a stand with the bus schedule on it, but it would do.

Finally alone, I sat down and pulled my mirror out to assess the damage. I looked awful, my makeup smudged, my mascara smeared, and my hair all over the show.

Sighing, I began fixing it, starting with my hair. Thankfully, I had my hairbrush and makeup tucked in my bag. On a good day I touched everything up after the karate lesson, but of course I hadn't had time. Might as well do it while I waited for the bus.

CHAPTER THREE

The bus hadn't come. At least not before I'd given up and begun walking home instead.

It was late enough the streets were now a bit quieter, and a part of me liked it that way. I'd walked them so often it was familiar, and it had given me time to think. I was going to have to find a new job as soon as possible, but with a reference I would probably be okay. With my check and the savings I had, I could survive for a couple of weeks. My situation wasn't as dire as I'd feared when I heard those dreaded two words.

The hard part would be finding something that worked with the karate lessons. It had been bad enough trying to get from my lesson to my job as it was. But it was the only other thing I had in my life. I trained and I taught, and I worked. It got me by, and it kept me from going crazy or hungry.

It also meant I didn't have to go back to my parents. Well, my adopted parents, anyway. I'd run away almost an entire decade earlier, hating the life I had there anyway. I hadn't fit in, and I'd disappointed my parents at every turn.

They were the wealthier end of middle class, quiet, reserved people. And I just... wasn't. I liked old heavy metal and grunge, and I wanted to dye my hair funky colors. I was better at drama and fighting than I was at math and English, and I hated being told what to do. During a big argument one day, it had all come out that I wasn't even theirs.

I ran away that night and I never looked back. For a year or so I slept on the streets in LA, not sure where the next meal was going to come from or how I was going to get by, but I managed to use what I knew to stay safe, and I made a tougher, bigger friend fast. That turned south when he wanted something for his protection.

I wasn't fooling around with someone just because he felt I owed him. Not long after that, I managed to get my first waitressing job. The place was a dive, and I suspected they'd been cooking the books by paying the staff under the table, but it got me off the streets, and I got my small apartment because of it.

It was there I was headed now. I'd stopped at a small store along the way, grabbing a microwave meal and a can of something that was supposed to be a cocktail already made up. Still several blocks out from my apartment, I noticed a sound behind me, followed by another, the two close enough together that they could have been footsteps.

But I was the only person who walked these streets that I would want to bump into.

I didn't look back yet, listening as I increased my speed

a fraction. Definite footfalls. Someone walking a little faster than me. Also alone. By sound alone I couldn't work out any more as I hurried along. I tried to catch a glimpse of who it might be in the reflections off car windows, but I either sucked at the movie technique or it didn't work the way movies made out it did, because I saw nothing.

With nothing else to do, I walked a little quicker again, also trying not to make much noise so I could listen, but the footsteps seemed to have died down or whoever it was had turned a different way. I frowned and dared look behind. There was no one there.

Sighing, I shook my head at my own paranoia. I knew I lived in a more dangerous area, but the regular folks came to know you. Left you alone once they considered you one of them. As long as you left them alone, anyway. And I'd been here long enough that a lot of them knew me. I'd served so many at one place or the other.

A retail job here, a waitress job there. Even a paper route at one point.

I'd only gone another hundred yards or so when the first drops of rain fell from the sky. I yanked up my hood and lifted the pace again. I didn't like being wet. I liked the sound of rain, especially thunderstorms. And tornadoes fascinated me, but I didn't like being wet. Never had.

My parents had said it was probably because I was found on a police station doorstep, the small box I was in starting to get soaked from the rain, the blanket around me no better.

Yeah, I was that kid, abandoned in a storm to the police. It was so cliché, I hadn't ever been able to bring myself to tell anyone. My usual story for those who had taken an interest in me was that I felt like I'd been adopted. They didn't need to know I knew I had. I wasn't lying. Long before I'd found out, I'd had the nagging doubt I didn't belong in my family or fit with them. But so did a lot of teenage girls, so I never thought much of it.

The rain grew harder as I walked, spilling down and pattering on nearby tin-roof garages until I was drenched. Shrinking into myself, I hurried along, splashing with every step.

It was only as I turned around the next corner, glancing behind by habit more than anything else, that I noticed someone behind me. The guy from the hotel. Mr. Hotel-Dinner was right behind me. Our eyes met for a fraction of a second before he darted straight at me. I lifted my arms to defend myself, but he didn't go for me, grabbing my bag instead.

His thin frame had so much momentum that he reacted far faster than I could, yanking my bag from my shoulder and spinning me as he did. It jarred my arm as the bag tore from my grasp. Before I knew what had happened, he was running off with it.

"Hey," I yelled as I sprinted after. Blinking against the rain, I followed him as best I could, but he was faster and already several yards ahead.

All my wages, my phone, and my karate kit were in that bag. Not to mention my apartment keys, dinner, and makeup. I couldn't lose that bag.

I didn't give up as my breath came in ragged gasps, my feet pounding. I'd said I was a sprinter, right? I wasn't built for this, but it was clear he was a sprinter too, his speed dropping after a while and his chest heaving with the intake of each breath. With any luck, I was fitter than he was, even if I sucked at long distance. I was desperate enough to catch him, that was for sure.

We went flying past the entrance to my apartment block, the thief no doubt having no idea I lived there, but I still wasn't gaining on him.

He glanced back a couple of times, his face appearing strange, almost like some kind of gnome or cat-like creature in a story as he did. Once more his eyes seemed to glow yellow, but I blinked and he was looking forward again, running.

Stretching out the lead he had on me, he darted down an unfamiliar alley. I hurried up to the corner as well, but when I turned to head down it, he was gone.

Shit! Shit, shit, shit, shit!

I was so completely screwed.

Everything of value had been in that bag. I walked down the alley anyway. The ache in my legs faded and the burning in my lungs turned to a dull roar that let me know I hadn't drunk enough for this kind of activity.

As I went further, dumpsters lining one side for a while, I heard a faint noise above the hammering of the rain. Hope filled me as I carried on. Had he hidden instead of running further? Was he here somewhere?

Or was I being lured into a trap? I didn't know, but I needed that bag. Maybe he'd ditch it once he had what he wanted. If nothing else, my apartment keys were vital.

I carried on, a little more cautious this time, pretty sure the noises were coming from further up. As I got to the last dumpster, I spotted him, crouched on the ground, stuffing things back into my bag.

"Hey!" I yelled, running close to grab it out of his hands. But as I came closer he threw it at me and then ran toward the road. I let out an oof at the weight of the bag as it hit me in the chest, but I caught it and cradled it to me for a moment.

Some of my makeup and my keys were still on the ground in a puddle, but otherwise I couldn't see anything else. I grabbed for both, groaning as I realized water had gotten into my eye shadow. That was ruined.

I rummaged through the rest of the bag, checking to see what he'd stolen. My fingers found my phone first, relief washing through me that he hadn't taken that. Probably thought it wasn't worth selling. I found my wages next, the packet containing all the cash I'd had left after I'd bought my dinner.

Creasing my forehead with confusion, I felt around the bag trying to work out what the strange man had taken. If I had my money, purse, keys, and phone, there was little else of value in there. Hunching over the bag to try to shield the contents from the rain, I rummaged further, checking each item of clothing as well. It was only as I pulled my hand out, ready to give up, that I realized my hairbrush was gone.

Had this guy just stalked me most of the way home and then assaulted me just so he could get my hairbrush?

Immediately I remembered his first comment at the diner. He'd asked if my hair was dyed. Was that why? Was he some kind of stalker with a hair fetish?

I shrugged, grateful either way. I was exhausted and had

no idea where I was, but I'd had my dinner, my phone, and what little money I had left was still tucked up in my bag.

For now, if some random stranger wanted to get off on my hairbrush, so be it. I had another at home. And I wouldn't be needing my karate kit one for a while if I didn't get another job soon. I couldn't afford the next month's payment for lessons if I didn't have an income. Not to mention I might not be able to even take the same classes.

Sighing, and grateful the rain was now easing off, I looked around to try to figure out where I was. It wasn't a set of buildings I recognized, so I took out my phone and pulled up the map I had on there. It showed the street behind me, where I'd come from, and the building to my left. But according to my map, the building on my right was meant to be a garden.

"Huh," I said aloud as I looked at it. In the dim evening and dull weather, it didn't look new. But the map was an up-to-date one. It should have known there was a building there. Had I just stumbled upon one of those government-owned secret places? A building that was meant to look like one thing, but wasn't?

More than a little curious, I walked down the side of the building, noticing that there was an alcove near the back, a light seeming to shine from it. When I got there I saw an open doorway, a definite glow coming from some-where inside.

The building itself was a concrete shell, an empty ware-house of sorts, a small room leading to a big open space. The glow seemed to move toward an old metal staircase at the far end. It wove back and forth on the far wall, before stopping at another open door. The inside of the door and the room beyond were lit with the same faint green glow. Whatever the source was, it was up there.

My feet moved toward it automatically. A couple of times as I approached I thought about the fact that I was trespassing, but the building was empty, not even a mouse scurrying along the skirting boards, and the door had been wide open. If someone wanted to keep people out, they shouldn't leave a place unlocked and doors open.

And they shouldn't leave lights on.

As I put my foot on the first rung of the stairs, I stopped. Did I really want to do this? Wasn't this how movie heroines got themselves killed? I shook the thought away. It was also how adventures began. And I was having a shitty enough day as it was. What could get worse? I'd keep listening, and if I heard anything, I could run away. Nothing was stopping me, and no one could get between me and the door. There was nowhere for them to hide.

Still, I climbed the stairs with gentle steps, not wanting to make a noise and alert anyone above me.

As I neared the top of the third flight, the glow faded, leaving me almost entirely in the dark. I carried on anyway, wondering what could have retreated like that and now so curious that I had to find an answer.

I was more cautious though, and I opted to carry my water bottle in one hand. It could act like a pretty sturdy weapon if I needed it to.

But there was no danger ahead. As I stepped into the room, I was met with yet more nothing.

The room was lit from a streetlamp at the front, enough spilling in through the window to give some shape to the area. It was partitioned off, like a set of cubicles, but I could see into all three. They were equally empty. At least... No... One of them had something in it.

The middle one, near the back, had a small wooden basket of some kind, and it appeared to have a very dull glow to it. A dull green glow. Sitting in the middle of the glow—or causing it; I wasn't sure which—was a lump. A lump that appeared to have scales.

Going closer, I realized it was egg shaped. It was a scaled egg, sitting in some kind of basket in the middle of nowhere, and it was definitely glowing with a dim light, as if it was hot.

Looking around, I tried to spot signs of a mother of some kind, an animal who might have laid the egg, but there wasn't anything. Not even a feather or any kind of reptile evidence. The egg was alone. Abandoned.

Immediately, I felt drawn to it. This was how my life had begun. A stranger finding me somewhere I shouldn't have been.

I shuffled even closer to the scaly egg, and the glow seemed to brighten a little, lighting up the palm of my hand just enough I could see to reach out and touch the egg. It didn't feel cold, but it wasn't very warm either.

Biting my lip, I wondered if it was already too cold to live, but as I reached for it with the other hand as well, there was a brief flash of light. Instantly, it felt warm to the touch.

I withdrew my hand, startled. For a fraction of a second, my handprint was outlined on the egg in a darker patch. Then the whole thing faded back to the deep brown color it had been before.

Taking several deep breaths to calm my racing heart, I decided I couldn't leave it. Whatever this strange object was, whatever creature lay inside, it had been forsaken here, and I wasn't going to leave it in the cold to die. My mind suggested a dragon, the scaled pattern reminiscent of those in fantasy books, but this was reality, not fiction. It couldn't be a dragon at all.

I picked up the basket and cradled it against me, finding the whole thing felt a little warmer again. As soon as I had a good grip on it, I made my way back to the stairs. I paused at the doorway to check the warehouse space below, but it was still empty. Just me and an egg in the entire building.

Despite knowing I was alone, I felt a strange desire to still be quiet as I went back down the stairs. I didn't want anyone to see my prize. To see what I'd discovered on my strange little adventure.

I thought of the man and the way he'd led me here. Had that been his intention? Did he know there was an egg in here. Had he seen the glow as well? I had so many questions, but I doubted any of them were going to be answered here.

As I reached the back door again, the rain had gone completely, but a cold breeze came whistling down the alley. Instantly, I looked to the egg and felt its temperature again. It felt warmer than ever, but I didn't want it to grow cold. Right there in the doorway, I took some of the stuff out of my bag, all the spare clothes except for my karate gi, and then I nestled the egg in the middle of the clothes.

"Sorry, it'll be a bit smelly," I said, putting everything

else into the basket I'd found the egg in so I could still carry everything home.

As soon as I was confident the egg would be warmer, I put the bag on top of the basket, not wanting to bump it against my body, and then I carried the lot like a proud mother hen, all the way back home.

CHAPTER FOUR

I sighed with relief as I placed the basket and bag onto the counter in my kitchen. Home at last.

For a moment I'd forgotten that I'd lost my job, so absorbed in the chaos that had happened since, but seeing the bills on the doormat on my way in had brought back all my needs. I had enough money to pay them, but it would wipe out what I'd just earned and then some.

Feeling deflated, I checked the egg's temperature for the hundredth time. It was getting hotter. When I first felt it, it had been colder than my body, although not by much. After it had flashed and I'd picked it up, it had felt a little warmer. Now it felt like the cozy temperature of a hot water bottle when you first get into bed.

Noticing the microwave meal as I lifted the bag out of the basket to put the egg somewhere safer, I heard my stomach rumble. I hadn't eaten anything in hours either.

I stuffed the meal in my microwave and put it on, then I turned my attention back to the egg. I still felt drawn to it, and ran my hands over the scales, marveling at how it still managed to have a sort of smoothness to its shell. They felt like rippling undulations rather than bumps and ridges. It was almost addictive, stroking it from top to bottom.

Having no idea what kind of animal laid an egg like this, I studied it in the kitchen light. It had appeared a dark greenish brown before, with a sort of faint glow to it, but now that I was somewhere brighter, I could see it was many different shades all together. I had to concentrate to pinpoint any one color, but it seemed to be made up of various shades of tan and ocher, and it even had flecks of a green here and there. It was stunning.

"And you're mine," I said, suddenly feeling like a mother hen with her most precious chick. Wanting to work out what it was, however, I pulled out my phone and took some photos.

By the time I'd finished getting the angles just right and taking a couple of photos I was happy with, my meal was cooked. I stuffed my phone in my top, grabbed a fork and slipped it into my mouth, tucked the bag and egg against my chest, and picked up the plate with my dinner with the other hand.

On the way through to my small living room and bedroom area, I clicked the light on with my elbow. For a moment I blinked, taking in the scene before me and trying to work out where to sit.

The curtains were still drawn from the night before. I'd been on a split shift that day and had left for the restaurant too early to bother opening them that morning. I hurried over to the small desk shoved in one corner, careful not to trip over the end of the bed as I did, and sank into my only chair.

Careful not to harm either, I put the egg in its makeshift nest on my lap and my meal to one side. As I started to eat the steaming mac and cheese, I powered on the computer.

Once again my eyes were drawn to what I'd found. The egg was so beautiful I could have stared at it for days. Was this what mothers meant when they said they could look at their babies all the time? I had no idea, but I almost laughed aloud at how silly I was being. It was just an egg. Some large eagle had probably laid it there and then been scared off by the traffic or something.

My computer was old and didn't work very well, so I'd eaten almost half my dinner by the time the thing was turned on and I could work with it. Turning on the internet, I told myself I could do a quick search to find out what creature had left the egg, and then if it wasn't one I could keep easily, or was on the exotic animals list, I could call an animal shelter that could deal with it and maybe release the creature back into the wild.

Then I could look for a new job. Because I was going to need one. *Especially if you're going to keep whatever hatches out*, my inner critic said. I rolled my eyes. Of course I wasn't going to keep it. But I imagined my apartment being more welcoming as I came home to a pet. And there was a pet store not far from the school I had karate lessons in.

Pushing my runaway thoughts away and trying not to get into an internal debate with myself, I searched for animals with scaled brown eggs. The first result gave me nothing but images of chicken eggs and tutorials for making fake dragon eggs. Not helpful.

I continued to search as I ate, trying every phrase, question, or search term I could think of. None of them helped. I just got back more confusing results.

"What are you?" I asked aloud when my food was long gone and I'd wasted almost half an hour trying to search more and more nuanced phrases.

There was no answer. Not that I'd expected one, but still. It didn't help me figure out what it was.

I sighed, touching it again to check how warm it was. It seemed to have reached a steady temperature now, warm and snug. And even the bag itself now felt warm around it. It gave me some confidence that at least I wasn't killing this strange unknown baby creature. Not sure what to do with it, I cuddled it while I checked my messages.

Not that long later, I thought I heard a strange tapping sound. Turning my gaze to my apartment, I looked for the source of the noise. I couldn't see anything and began to feel silly, until I realized it came from the egg. The creature inside the egg was trying to hatch.

Already?

I gulped, nerves telling me that I wasn't sure I was ready for whatever was inside to come out, but there wasn't much I could do about it. If I hadn't wanted this thing to hatch, I shouldn't have brought it home with me. I did, however.

Whatever was inside this egg, it was special. And I wanted to make sure it was going to live a long, happy life.

No sooner had I thought this than a crack appeared, the sound of the shell breaking so loud the neighbors might have heard it. The tapping continued for a few more minutes before something inside seemed to sigh and relax again for a moment. I wondered if the creature had worn itself out trying to get that far, so I stroked the outside and talked to it in a low voice.

"It's okay, little one. You're in a safe place now. I'm going to take care of you," I whispered before I thought about what I was doing. I'd expected to feel silly saying these kinds of things, but I didn't. I felt calm. It felt right. In a way life hadn't, and shouldn't, given I'd just lost my job. Maybe I needed a break from the crazy rat race that was earning enough just to pay bills and buy food.

The egg either agreed with my thoughts or was grateful for the encouragement, because I'd have sworn it got a little brighter. But the tapping didn't resume.

"But I still don't know what you are," I said. "And I'm going to need to get you food, or something for when you hatch, aren't I?"

There was no response, but I nodded for it. All baby creatures were hungry little things. While I sat there I did a mental checklist of foods I had in the house. I had some sausages in the fridge, as well as some wilting salad, but that covered two bases. I thought there were even a couple of overripe bananas in the fruit bowl.

It would suffice, but I had a feeling my baby eggbert would need something more nutritious going forward, and if I was going to have any chance of getting it right, identifying him or her asap would help.

Remembering the photos I'd taken, I decided to see if the world of social media could help me. Maybe someone would know a specialist vet, or a friend of a friend who worked for a zoo. And I'd met and interacted with a lot of people over the years. With some sharing and the beauty of the egg's scales, I didn't doubt I'd generate some buzz. With any luck it would be the kind that got me answers.

Within a minute the photos were up and I was already getting reactions and comments.

No one knew what it was, but they all agreed it was beautiful. I hadn't mentioned it was already hatching. No one needed to know I might be about to get eaten by some giant bird or snake when it hatched out in my apartment. I was pretty sure snake eggs were a lot more slimy and smaller, however.

I did a quick internet search to be sure, but I was only partway through when my computer crashed.

Shitsticks.

I sighed as the creature started tapping again, pushing at the shell where it had cracked and making it crack further. I couldn't look away, wondering if it was going to break out this time, but it gave up again, having made the original two cracks bigger, and added another small one running in a third direction.

"Don't worry, little guy," I said. "You'll be out of there in no time."

Yawning, I moved to the bed with it. It was getting late, I'd gotten up early, and I couldn't be bothered to figure out what had crashed my computer. It was a heap of junk anyway.

As I settled in for the night, curling myself up around the bag with my homemade nest in, I grabbed my phone to see if anyone else had commented. In no time at all, I pulled up the stream and flicked through, trying to find the pictures and all the comments, but they were all gone.

Growling my frustration at two pieces of tech borking

in such a short space of time, I decided to post them again. I needed to know what this egg was. When I tried to post again, however, I found the photos were also gone from my phone.

This made me sit up a little more. Everything had been working fine until I'd posted photos of the egg, and now my computer had crashed, my social media had been wiped of them, and the photos were gone from my phone. Two of those was a stressful coincidence. All three rang alarm bells. Had someone just hacked my stuff?

Was this egg something important? Instantly I thought back to the building I'd found it in. It hadn't been on the map. Had I just stolen an animal from some super-secret government project?

I bit at my lip, unable to shake the idea. As the egg continued to tap and rattle, this time wobbling a little, even more cracks appeared and grew. I knew I couldn't sleep until I'd thought this through.

If this was something the government had created, then they were likely to want it back. But as I pictured giving it to some official dressed in a lab coat, I knew there was no way I was going to want to just hand it over. It felt like it was mine. My handprint had appeared on it.

But was I willing to run off with it?

Until I knew what was inside, I knew I couldn't give it back. But I did the few things I could think of to keep safe. I turned my phone off, pulling open the back and taking the battery out so no one could hack it and use it to listen in, then I tucked it in the bag as well. With that done, I padded through to the kitchen to fetch my purse and the rest of the stuff I kept in my bag.

I'd left all of it sitting in the basket, and only as I approached now did I bother to take in what it was made of. The basket was a light sort of wood that was also incredibly strong. The outside was carved and varnished a deep brown color that complimented the egg itself. And the pictures carved into the edges were so detailed and smooth they looked like a work of art.

Dragons flew across mountains and forests, each one with a rider on their backs, shooting something out of their hands. A mini tornado whirled on the ground here and there, almost as if they were part of some epic battle.

It wasn't clear why someone would have carved something like that for an egg basket, but I felt a pang of sadness that the egg wasn't in it. Whoever had made it had taken the time to do so, and that probably meant the egg was important to them too. Pulling everything out of my bag again and being careful to keep the egg wrapped in my gi, I tried to see if the basket would fit inside. It didn't.

Sighing, I took my time over repacking the bag, making sure it had everything in it I would need if I had to run from the government, because it seemed that at least subconsciously I had made my decision. I wasn't giving it up without a fight.

I shook my head at myself as I thought about such a crazy idea, but carried on anyway. Then I took the basket and went to the bed with it. I had one of those beds with drawers underneath. I'd found out a long time ago that the drawers didn't take up the space under all of it. Just most of it.

The basket was just thin enough I should be able to fit it in behind them.

"There," I said as I got back up again, the basket hidden. That will have to do.

Yawning, I got back in the bed. With the bag once more curled up against my stomach, I tried to rest. The egg didn't look like it was going to hatch just yet, but either way, I needed sleep.

If the government was going to come here, I figured they'd be here in a hurry. I just had to listen out for a lot of cars stopping suddenly outside. And I always slept with the window ajar. This high up no one was climbing in, but it meant I'd hear. Hopefully it would wake me.

CHAPTER FIVE

A loud cracking sound disturbed my dozing. I hadn't been sleeping in more than a few-minute bursts, every car noise and every tap and crack keeping me from settling properly.

I was about to roll over, carefully moving my egg nest, when I heard a strange noise, and several cars pulled up at once. My eyes went wide open. A moment later I looked toward the window. Lights shone up at it, flicking back and forth. Flashlights?

I didn't know, but a flood of adrenaline pumped through my body, making me wide awake in seconds. I sat up, careful not to tip my bag. A moment later I picked up on the sounds of voices and people gathering outside.

No matter who that was, I'd had enough of being paranoid. Not waiting around to find out if they'd all come for me, I grabbed the bag and shifted it over before I found the nearest set of non-work pants and pulled them on.

I was dressed and wearing shoes in less than two minutes. On the way past my desk, I grabbed my usual hairbrush and shoved it into my bag, tucking it down beside the egg, then I hurried to the door, via the kitchen. I grabbed a few snack bars and anything quick to eat before checking the hallway through the spyhole on the door.

No one was there, but something made me sure they would be soon. Like a sixth sense or a premonition, I just knew people were here for me and the egg. I grabbed the chain on the door and unlocked it, pulling it shut behind me and also shoving the keys in the bag. I then yanked the drawstring a little tighter, but not so tight I couldn't see the crack in the egg and the small hole the baby creature had made.

I rushed toward the back set of stairs, not trusting the front. There would be more people there than I liked, and I was sure they would be fanning out by now.

Going down the stairs as silently as I could, I listened for sounds. I heard the telltale squeak of the bottom floor door to the hallway and almost froze. Only the sound of people coming up the stairs after that, rushing and not trying to hide their noise, made me move again.

I hurried down the flight I was on and tucked into the corridor off that, waiting out of sight for whoever was going up to go past and hoping they were making straight for my floor.

My hunch was rewarded when I heard them all clatter past. It sounded like four of them going up this set of stairs. I didn't doubt there would be more at the other end of the building as well.

As soon as I was pretty sure it was safe, I came out of my hiding place and continued down the steps again. This time I didn't go quite so quickly, but I didn't delay either. Just enough so I could pad and muffle my steps. It was important they didn't realize I was trying to leave until the last possible moment.

I reached the bottom without further incident, but I carried on, going even slower, to the nearby door. Outside were two men watching the doorway. I could just see their shadows on the pavement. Retreating into the bottom floor of the apartment block, I looked for an alternate route out, but I came up blank. They were bound to be guarding the front.

Pausing for a moment, I tried to think of the best way out. I just couldn't be sure. I knew I couldn't handle too many of them, but I had been training and studying martial arts ever since I had arrived in LA. Could I beat a couple of them? I had a feeling I was going to need to find out. But instead of feeling sick or apprehensive, I felt myself almost seem to grow on the inside somewhere. Like I had been born for this.

I could do this.

I knew I had to try. I couldn't let my egg go back wherever they were trying to take it.

Not thinking about it any longer, I walked to the nearby electricity cupboard. Before I could pull it open, I heard an almighty bang come from somewhere higher up in the middle. Somewhere toward my own apartment.

They're trying to break in, I thought, gritting my teeth. They would soon discover I wasn't in there. As another bang sounded, I yanked open the cupboard door, grateful for the noise shielding my own actions. The inside of the small cupboard was nice and warm and made me feel a little better about abandoning my bag and the egg in there, even momentarily.

"I'll be back for you in just a few minutes," I said, tucking it behind an abandoned pushchair.

I shut the door again as gently as I could and then strode toward the outer door.

Please don't have guns, I thought as I walked closer. But I was soon disappointed to notice they did. Two men, as I'd suspected, were watching the back door, and both of them carried a pistol of some kind. Guns had never been a strong point of mine, but neither of them aimed one at me as I came out. I looked between them.

Both men wore suits, and had dark sunglasses and blank expressions. Whoever they were, they were some kind of government something, or dressed to look like it.

"I don't want any trouble," I said, trying to act as if they weren't there for me. "I just need to get to work."

They looked to each other briefly, and I took the break in eye contact as a sign that I could come past them. Walking quickly, I tried not to make eye contact again, but get out of their way.

I was going to have to disable them, but there was no doubt I couldn't do it while they were waving guns around unless I could be sure they wouldn't shoot.

They parted to let me through, appearing to believe my bluff, but as soon as I was level with them, their radios sprang to life. Whoever was in charge inside the apartment block was letting them know I wasn't there.

I grabbed the gun of the suited man on my left and twisted it, turning my body as I did. He refused to let go of his weapon, but that just gave me the momentum to flip him over, crouch, and drive the gun down into his face. It smashed his nose, making him loosen the grip long enough for me to yank it away and stand again.

Looking toward the second man, I saw he was grabbing for his radio, his mouth open and his gun aiming in my rough direction but not with much precision.

Feeling calmer than I ought to and just reacting, I kicked out at his gun hand. The weapon went flying, not held well enough to benefit him anymore, and he dropped his radio too.

As I put my foot down, I put both hands on the grip of the pistol I'd stolen and aimed it at him. I didn't like how it felt in my hands, but I glanced at it long enough to know it had a safety of sorts. I wasn't about to shoot him, and he hadn't been about to shoot me. At least I wasn't being totally reckless with my life.

"Don't answer that radio," I said. "In fact, hand it over. Carefully."

The man gulped but took his time to bend and pick the device up. He took it out of the belt holster as he handed it to me. It was a pretty simple radio, so I stuffed it into the front pocket on my sweatshirt and then tried to decide what to do. I couldn't actually shoot this guy, but I knew I had to get the egg and get out of here.

"Turn around," I said, still not sure what I was doing, but trying to make things work nonetheless. Thankfully he complied, shaking as he did. Did he really think I might hurt him?

Stepping forward, I smacked him over the back of the head with the gun, knocking him out as his partner tried to rise, still clutching his face. I shoved him back over as well, the first hitting the ground with a thud, and the second letting out an oomph as I winded him.

Throwing the gun as far into the nearby bushes as I could, I sprinted back to the building and hauled the door open again. Then I darted to the electricity cupboard. No sooner had I gotten it open than I heard footsteps on the stairs again. I had more attackers coming my way. I grabbed the bag, trying to both be careful and quick, and cradled it to me.

The egg inside looked like it might have cracked open more since I'd left it but I couldn't be sure and wasn't about to stick around to find out. I sprinted back to the door again, only stopping to turn my body and push it open with my side.

Swiveling back to face the right way as the door swung shut behind me, I saw the guy with the smashed-up face lying on the floor and talking into the radio in his hand.

On the way past, I booted it out of his hands, hearing a crunch and a yelp. I winced as I realized I'd probably done as much damage to the hand holding it as I had the device itself.

"Sorry," I said, as he tried to rise again and lash back out at me. I twisted myself around, feeling his hands try to get a grip on my jacket, but I was too fast. After slipping out of his grasp, I ran as fast as I could away.

Out the back of the apartment block, they'd tried to make a green space. Somewhere kids could play. But it had been ruined in days by alcoholics and drug addicts using it as a quiet place to shoot up or just hide from those who would give them lectures or try to stop them getting high again.

As such, it was littered with rubbish, needles, and broken glass. Plus it stank. I was used to it, however, and knew the best route through it. I needed to get away from these men and lead them through a maze, so I darted down the next alley, my feet pounding hard as my breath grew ragged. The radio in my pocket was going nuts, but I was making too much noise and it was partially smothered between me and the bag. I couldn't make out much, other than "suspect" and "running."

Yup, that was me. I was running. In less than half a day, I'd gone from being a respectable martial arts student and waitress to a wanted fugitive on the run for stealing some unidentified creature.

And I had never felt more alive.

Before I could get to the end of the alley, however, I could hear shouts and heavy boots pounding on the concrete. I tried to push myself faster, feeling the wind pick up and almost push me forward. I was right at the end of the alley when two more suits came out of nowhere and blocked it.

Going too fast to slow down, I put my hand out, trying to protect the egg I carried and not crush it between me and them.

"Don't break it!" I yelled, trying to slow anyway.

Either something pushed them back or they listened and backed off, I couldn't tell which, their movements seeming unnatural, but their expressions masked by the sunglasses they also wore.

Wondering how they saw in the darker light of early morning, I kicked out at the nearest one, both arms holding the bag and egg close to me. This guy was a bit more prepared for fighting and dodged several times, but it was clear they didn't want to hurt the egg either as both hesitated about fighting back.

"Stop her," someone yelled from behind. "And get that bag."

I felt rather than saw the other guy lunge for the bag and latch onto the fabric, but I gripped the straps and top section even tighter and spun once more. His momentum in the same direction helped topple him over my foot, and he had a split second to choose between using his hands to save his fall, or trying to keep hold of the bag.

He picked the latter, but all it seemed to do was spin him, so he hit the ground with the side of his arm and shoulder. There was another crunch, the arm dislocating. He still didn't let go of the bag.

Acting on impulse, I stamped on his arm and then flung myself in the other direction. It made him let go of the bag, and I carried on. The final man stood in my way though, hands empty, glancing more than once at the bag I carried. I feinted one way and then the next before he reached out to try to grab at it. Once more I spun, dodging as I did and sticking my foot out.

He tripped right over the stuck-out appendage and went sprawling.

I didn't wait or attack any further, the first already getting back to his feet and more men running down the alley. Instead, I rushed onward. My legs were burning and each breath reminded me how dry my mouth was. I needed to get somewhere safer, and fast, but my body didn't slow, the wind once more joining with me and almost pushing me along.

Up ahead I caught the welcome sight of a bus stop, complete with a couple of early-shift workers, no doubt heading downtown to open a shop or cafe for breakfast.

The world had begun to lighten as I'd been running, and I could just make out movement as the bus came trundling up and stopped. I glanced and saw the men were a hundred yards or so behind, and the bus a couple of hundred ahead.

I pushed myself to run like I never had before.

Please be the driver who is in a hurry and won't wait for the men chasing me, I thought as the last person got on and began paying when I was only thirty yards away. I slowed for the last bit, using one hand to grab the front of the bus and turn myself.

I bumped the far door with my side a little before I was on. Reaching straight into the side of my bag, I pulled out my whole wad of cash.

"Keep the extra. Just hurry up. I'm late to an interview," I lied as I put down all the coins I had in the bus driver's hands. He glanced at them a moment before pushing the button to shut the doors.

Within another second, we were pulling off.

"Where are you headed to?" he asked as he got back into his lane and reached for his ticket yards. I paused for a moment. I didn't want to go too far, or I was sure they'd have more men on the stops ahead, but I needed to go far enough, and somewhere I could hide.

"Just to the hub," I replied. "Return ticket."

"Then you gave me far too much," he replied, not taking his eyes off the road.

"Yeah, as I said, I need to get to this job interview. I was fired from my last job."

"We've all been there, cupcake. I'll do my best, but this thing doesn't have many speeds."

"Beats walking." I exhaled, beginning to get my breath back and feeling the ache recede from my chest and legs. Careful not to jolt my burden, I made my way to the nearest seat and sat down.

There were only a handful of others on the bus, and no one was paying me any attention, everyone with their heads in phones or books, most also listening to music. I pulled back the drawstring on my bag a little to get a better look and checked that my cargo had made it through the fight safely.

More of the top of the egg had cracked off, revealing a little of the animal inside. It looked like a ridge of some kind on a nose. A glistening deep brown nose, almost bronze-like in its shine and smoothness. Whatever was inside the egg, it was going to be beautiful.

CHAPTER SIX

Trundling along on the bus, I focused on the scenery around me and the familiar streets of LA, grateful when the bus hub came in sight. It didn't take long, the driver true to his word and getting me there as quickly as he could.

I felt a lot calmer now that I'd had a chance to sit for a minute, and it seemed I wasn't the only one who had picked up on the opportunity. While I'd sat on the bus the creature had tapped away again, drawing a glance or two from a nearby passenger. The egg had cracked open even further, and I could see inside a little better.

The bronze coloring continued on down the creature's nose, its texture as scaly as the egg itself. It was a reptile. For a moment I felt nervous. Would it be a vicious creature? I had no way to tell, but just in case, it was time to get me and it out of the vicinity of others.

There was an abandoned mall not too far from the stop, and I headed straight for it as soon as I'd got off the bus. The driver wished me good luck and I hesitated before I thanked him, forgetting for a moment that I had told him I was going for an interview.

Feeling the ache return to my legs as I hurried along, I tried not to worry. With the strange stalker who had stolen my hairbrush the night before, and the running I'd done to catch him, all the extra walking to and from work, and now the early-morning sprint today, I was feeling the effects. But I had no idea if I was safe or not.

The mall wasn't far, however, the front of it shuttered, covered in graffiti. Many of the glass panes into the building were broken and had been boarded up, but I'd spent several months on the streets; I knew what to look for.

The second board from the far left had a slightly different angle to it. It was subtle. A normal person prob-ably wouldn't notice. Looking around to check no one saw me, I walked up to it and pushed at the edges. The bottom right gave the tiniest fraction, and then I could slide the panel to the left, and squeeze through the gap, bag first.

As I pushed the panel closed behind me, I waited for a moment for my eyes to adjust. I wouldn't be alone in here, but I was in the kind of place no one would want to turn me in to any kind of authority. Everyone here was likely to be wanted for something, or wanting to hide from a world they thought little of.

It was also possible some of the people here would be faces I knew, but either way, I didn't plan on bothering anyone or getting too close. I just needed to find a nice empty-looking shop and tuck myself away for a bit.

Quite a few of the ones nearest the door had been trashed, some of them even burned and broken, so I headed deeper. I didn't want to go too deep on the first floor, the back housing a drug dealer, so I hiked up the broken escalator, careful not to get my feet caught in the torn slats. It was always strange that things like this were ruined so quickly, but some people seemed to like to destroy stuff. And they didn't care how many others their destruction inconvenienced.

It wasn't long before I reached the next floor, however. Immediately, I noticed quite a few shops with lights in—flashlights, candles, and fairy lights providing most of the light—and the sound of voices as people conversed in hushed tones. Here was the floor a lot of the homeless were living on. I carried on up again to the top floor. The mall wasn't very big, especially for this kind of city, and I could only assume it had gone bust, but a part of me right now was more than a little grateful for its existence.

The mall going under had put a fair few people out of work, but someone had since built an even bigger, newer one down the street. That was how America worked. The old, even if not that old, was forgotten about for the newest shiny. You knew it was the beginning of the end when all the trendy shops started moving their premises to the new mall.

The third floor was far quieter, but that didn't mean it was empty. Others, like me, seeking to stay out of the way, would have come up here. And I didn't want to bother those kinds of people as much as I didn't want them to bother me.

Looking at the shop entrances, I chose one that had been pushed open, but only just. I could just about squeeze through the gap, but not many others would. I'd have to remove the bag too, but I needed to check it was safe first.

Getting closer without making any noise, I listened out for sounds of an occupant. After a few seconds, I was satisfied that if anyone was in there they were going to be as cautious as I was. I looked under the gap, but the inside was dark, no one lighting it up from inside.

Frowning, I tried to think of a light source I could use. I didn't have one. Where could I find something?

Straightening again, I looked for a shop that might still have something in that could be used. It was a long shot, but this floor looked more intact than others, and as if the last few shops who'd appeared to abandon their wares hadn't been fully looted yet.

I moved further into the mall, finding something others might have overlooked. A little gift shop, most often carrying tacky souvenirs. This wasn't a great place for it, out of the way on the top floor of the mall, but the shutter had been broken into and bent back. It was clear goods still sat inside, although some lay smashed on the floor.

As the sun was coming up outside, it grew a little easier to see inside the units, the skylight above doing its job, but I still had to be careful as I stepped inside.

Once again, the shop was quiet, but I had a good look around anyway for the telltale mound of a person huddled under a coat, or if they were lucky, a sleeping bag. I couldn't see one from where I stood, but I continued to move carefully. The first sets of shelves contained cheap Hollywood signs, most broken or discolored as if water had leaked on them.

I carried on, hearing the occasional crunch as I stepped

on the broken remnants of something I couldn't see in the dark. Despite the strange place I was in, I felt calm, my focus on my task—finding something that would light up.

Eventually I found it. Near the back of the store, where I'd eased along and felt my way in the dark. One of those garish light-up ties. It wasn't a lot of light, but there were more of them. I stripped the insides out of several, using the light and batteries of the first few to see, and then I clutched a handful and carried on. Ideally I wanted something brighter, and something a more neutral color, but it didn't take me long with the aid of the extra light to find a box of light-up Liberty statues.

It was the wrong state, but it seemed everyone liked Lady Liberty. Beside the statues, in the same box, were lighters and all sorts of other themed items. I pocketed a couple of lighters and grabbed a handful of statues as well.

Between them, it was progress, and would probably be bright enough for now.

I was considering having a look for other items when I felt the bag sort of wriggle and the egg crack some more. I had a feeling that I didn't have much time, so I hurried back to the store I'd chosen for my hideout and checked the inside out for a second time with the added benefit of being able to see. The store's inside looked untouched, the shelves empty but with plenty of space for someone to hide and make a sort of nest.

Feeling more than a little relieved to have a space I could call my own for a while, I eased the bag off my shoulders and down to the floor, aware the creature was pushing at the egg. Another bit cracked off as I crouched. Hurrying, I slid under the gap, pulling the bag after me.

I fitted under fine, but the bag and egg almost got stuck. It took me a moment to ease everything under and then I merely pulled the bag, statues and fairy lights further back and behind the customer service desk so I couldn't easily be seen from the outside. Then, I waited.

I hadn't felt nervous at all before, so it took me completely by surprise to feel things now. I grew tense and couldn't tear my eyes away, an equal mix of terrified, curious, and eager to see what came out of this egg, especially after everything I'd done to keep it.

You're mad, girl, my alter ego kindly told me. *You've thrown everything away and you don't even know what for.*

Not the first time, I quipped back. I'd run away from everything once already. It wasn't like I had enjoyed my life or was attached to it.

This silenced my inner critic and I settled down to watch and murmur further encouragement. The creature finally pushed through the shell about half an hour after I had curled up with it, and a head emerged.

It was a reptilian face, two small horns protruding from the head and a longish, almost crocodile-like snout, although it was scaled differently, tougher looking and shinier. Two forward-facing eyes fixed on my face.

I blinked a couple of times lazily. I'd read somewhere that you did the same if you wanted a cat to like you. That the lazy blinking identified you as not being threatened or threatening. Last thing I wanted to do was make this baby feel threatened. Equally, I didn't want it to attempt to eat me either.

Two small three-pronged claws reached up and pushed at more of the eggshell, breaking it off until it could wriggle its body and emerge from the shell. I gasped as I noticed two webbed wings come out from either side of its body, followed by another couple of legs and a long tail, more buds of ridges and spikes evident trailing down its back and tail.

I was holding a dragon. A bronze dragon.

But dragons didn't exist. Did they?

"Hi," I whispered, not sure what else to do as the creature regarded me. It seemed to tilt its head to the side and look at me.

"I'm Aella-Faye," I said a moment later. "I found you all alone. Would you like me to take care of you?"

It blinked, almost lazily. Was it copying what I had done earlier? I had no idea so I did the same, exaggeratedly slowly. A moment later it copied me.

Beginning to grin, we kept up a cycle of slow blinks until I was chuckling every time it copied me. On the seventh or eighth blink it did, it let out a deep throaty rumble.

"Did you just laugh?" I asked, but it tilted its head to the side. "I guess you don't understand me."

It looked at me again, and then it turned its gaze elsewhere. It took its time to examine the bag, the shop, and then focused back on me. As soon as it had my attention, the creature opened its jaw, leaned forward a bit, and snapped it shut.

"Uhhh..." I replied, no clue what it was trying to ask, but then as it did it again, understanding hit me. It was hungry.

I very slowly reached down into the pack beside it, pushing bits of eggshell aside until my hand closed on the first of my snacks. A packet of salami. I pulled it out, equally careful not to be too jerky or sudden, but the dragon didn't move, watching as I went.

As I opened the packet, the dragon started sniffing the air, leaning toward it. Its eyes seemed to light up and its mouth fell open, almost drooling on me as I held out the sausage-shaped meat.

It snapped a bit off the end, appearing to be careful not to get my fingers, something I was very grateful for, and quickly chomped it down. In less than ten seconds I was down to the last piece. I held it in the palm of my outstretched hand, hoping it wouldn't bite me as it tried to get the rest of the meat.

Carefully it stretched forward again and bit the end of the piece. Then it flicked it up into the air a little, catching it on the way back down. With what looked like the tiniest of chews and a big swallow, the salami was all gone.

It rippled out its wings and let out a small *rawrl* noise before looking to me again.

"Did you like that?" I asked.

It snapped its jaws again and then looked down into the bag around it.

"You want more?" I frowned. There wasn't much more. I hadn't planned on having a hungry dragon in my bag, or eating my food, the last time I'd been shopping. I didn't have any more meat at all, but I did have a few other packaged snacks. I reached in, being careful and slow again, and pulled out the snack bars I had. I also had a banana in there and some nuts.

The dragon watched me but waited as I opened the snack bar. It sniffed it but only took a tentative bite, breaking off a small piece. I watched and waited, but it tilted its head to the side and swallowed before snorting and shaking its head as it bounced its front claws up and down.

"Right. Didn't like that one then," I said, taking a bite of the rest. Immediately my mouth watered and my stomach gurgled. I was a lot hungrier than I'd realized.

"What about fruit?"

I tried everything else I had, but the dragon would do no more than eat a little bit. When I'd offered it some of everything, it ate the rest of the banana, but it was almost reluctant, as if it would have preferred more of the salami.

Frowning, I snacked on the rest. I now had a hungry dragon to look after, and it was going to want more food. But how was I going to get some for it?

Before I could think of an answer, it decided it had had enough of sitting in my bag, and turned to look around itself again. A moment later, it hopped onto the floor. At first the little creature was unsteady on its legs, its body about the same size as a small cat. I marveled at how it had fit inside the egg, but I supposed it had been curled up tightly.

It seemed to enjoy sniffing around the empty shop, checking out my lights before bounding up onto one of the shelves. A few times it stretched its wings, but it didn't attempt to fly.

Still feeling a little stunned at what I'd found, but now no longer surprised government agents of some kind were after me, I trailed the dragon around the shop like a mother watching her child explore a park for the first time.

CHAPTER SEVEN

"Rawrl," the dragon said for the fifth time in only ten minutes. I was pretty sure it was hungry again.

"All right," I replied. "I'll try to get you some food."

I looked toward my bag, trying to decide whether I should leave the dragon here and go to get groceries alone or try to encourage the creature back into the bag to take with me.

As I reached into my bag and tidied up the eggshell pieces, marveling at how smooth and how beautiful the broken pieces were, the dragon came closer again.

I pulled out some money next and tucked a twenty dollar bill into my pants pocket before I assessed what else I needed. Most of the food was gone, just two more snack bars and a few nuts left, and my water bottle was now empty. I'd drunk most of it, but the dragon had lapped a little out of the bottle cap. We both needed more water for sure, and my new charge needed food.

As I went to pull the drawstring on the bag and leave the dragon behind, figuring it would be safer here, it seemed to sense my intentions. Immediately it let out the same little growl, this time deeper, more aggressive sounding. I decided the dragon was a boy.

Letting go of the bag, I turned to look at him, but he was already wriggling and eyeing the bag. He leaped into it, tangling a foot on the string and splatting onto the middle.

Sighing at the mess he'd made of the leap but still grinning, I reached down and carefully helped him untangle his clawed back foot. The moment he was free and upright again, he snuggled back down into the bag as if it were a nest of sorts. Then he looked at me and glanced at the exit.

"Well, for someone that's only been hatched an hour, you're a clever little thing," I said, easing the bag up and carrying it to the shutter. "But you're going to have to stay out of sight. Most people have never seen a dragon before."

Until today that included you, my alter ego pointed out. I mentally stuck my tongue out at her and looked out under the shutter. No sign of anyone, but the day looked to be bright and no doubt the shops would all be open by now. I just needed to find a store that sold some more packaged meat and some water.

Maybe a sandwich and some lunch for you too, my alter ego added as I shuffled myself back underneath the shutter and out into the open.

Good thought, I replied, at least grateful for that.

"Rawrl," the dragon added from inside the bag. I paused for a moment. Had he just replied to my thoughts, or was he checking he'd not been left behind? I didn't know, but it was probably just a coincidence. Either way, I took my time and eased him under the metal gateway as well, careful not to catch him on it, but he seemed to understand and hunkered down into the bag to make it easier.

As soon as we were both on the other side, I lifted the straps and tucked the bag across my torso again. I pulled the drawstring a little more closed, gently pushing his head below the top when he tried to lift it up and look out.

"You have to stay hidden, remember?"

He huffed out a burst of air but settled down. Gratitude at his ability to understand my words already swept through me as I made my way toward the escalators. I knew I looked a little strange carrying my bag on my front, but I'd just appear to be a tourist. It wasn't uncommon in a place like LA for people to carry their belongings where they could see them.

Of course, it could actually increase the chances a person was pickpocketed, making it very obvious you were a tourist, but I felt certain that if anyone tried to steal from me now, they would get one big surprise. I had a guard dragon sitting on top of my phone and purse.

Our eyes met, and he blinked slowly. Chuckling as I did the same, I made my way to the bottom floor.

I could hear more people moving about, especially on the second floor, but the one person I saw, a woman who looked to be in her thirties, took one fleeting look at me and carried on.

Within another minute I was outside, managing to squeeze us both through the gap by the right board without too much difficulty.

In this quiet part of town no one seemed to notice me get out of the abandoned mall, but that was just the first hurdle. I had to stay inconspicuous while I also found food.

Keeping to the backstreets, and away from the major tourist locations, I made my way toward the only shop I could think of nearby that would sell what I needed.

I looked about me frequently, knowing there were plenty of cops on foot, in cars and other authority figures in the area. I didn't know if the cops would be looking out for me, but I didn't want to take the chance.

Blending in as I expected, I sighed with relief each time anyone who did see me treated me like a tourist. Someone even asked if I was lost when I walked down a back road. I shook my head, not trusting my voice, as I carried on. Every few yards I glanced down, aware of the dragon riding in my bag.

Looking around me, I tried to spot any potential dangers but for the most part I was in the middle of LA and everyone was too busy going about their day to pay me much attention.

My shoulders ached a little and my legs were little better, but I carried on. I was also pretty parched and I didn't know how much food and water the dragon would need, but I didn't want to make him go hungry. Who knew what a starving dragon might do?

More than a little tense, my heart rate up and my breathing more rapid than normal, I felt like I'd been for a run as I reached the nearest food store. I'd only traveled about half a mile, but it had felt far longer, my body constantly on alert for danger.

The second I stepped into the store I relaxed a little, and walked up the first aisle. It took me a moment to find the cold meats, but they had some more packaged salami and other snacks I liked. It didn't take me long to realize I was going to want a basket. With no idea how much the dragon might eat, I planned on getting plenty.

Keeping track of how much money I was spending as I went, I used up the entire twenty-dollar bill.

As I dumped the food down on the counter, I tried not to show how nervous I felt. The dragon wriggled several times as I waited for it all to be rung up, then I handed over my cash and grabbed everything.

Not taking a bag, I shoved the water bottles in the outside pouch on my bag and then balanced everything else in my arms. Stepping outside, I looked around again. I froze as I saw a cop car pulled to a stop just outside the store. Was it there for me?

But the cop in question walked straight past me from behind, heading to the car with a drink and a sandwich of his own.

I hurried away, not wanting to give him or anyone else a chance to identify me, and then I found another alley to hide in as my dragon started to wriggle and move about more and more.

More than a little irritated that he wouldn't wait for me to get back to the mall, or somewhere else safe, I hid behind a dumpster, grateful it didn't smell too much.

As soon as I stopped moving the dragon lifted his head up, poking it out of the top of the bag and sniffing around. The second his eyes fixed on the salami, he tried to claw up and out of the bag.

I sighed and ripped the pack open. Within seconds the first salami was gone and he was nudging my hand with his nose to get me to open another.

Not quite sure I could believe what I was seeing, I

watched as the dragon ate everything I'd bought for him, and still eyed my sandwich. I frowned and pulled it away from him.

"This one is mine," I said, having intended to save it for later, but the dragon continued to sniff at it. I'd bought a BLT, one of my favorites, but I clearly wasn't going to get all of it. As I opened it, the dragon pushed the lettuce away with his claws and pulled out the bacon.

I sighed, watching it eat the best bit of the whole sandwich, not sure I could stop him even if I wanted to.

"Great," I said as he sat back in the bag and let out a burp. "Just eat my food too."

He lowered his head, but seemed to grin up at me, almost like he was only half ashamed of himself.

"You're a cheeky little shit," I said, but inside, a part of my heart melted. He was clearly my cheeky little shit.

I munched on the rest of the sandwich as I opened the water bottle and let him try to lap some out. He spilled some of that too, but soon we were both full and no longer thirsty.

With our immediate needs met, I tucked him back into the bag. We had to find somewhere to lie low for a while. And I needed to work out what we were going to do about our future.

There was no way I was going to let the government have their dragon back. The very fact a dragon existed, and they were trying to hide him from the world, made me feel protective.

Or worse, alter ego pointed out.

Or worse, I agreed.

Sighing, I decided I needed to head back to the mall. At

least there I'd had a place I could relax and think, but I was clearly going to need more food first. Not daring to go back to the same shop and look suspicious by buying up even more of their meat, I opted to go to the one other place I knew would sell what I needed and wasn't too far away. Grand Central Market.

The vendors sold all sorts of things there, and I'd stand out less too. With any luck, looking like a tourist would help me blend into a crowd.

As I hurried along, once again trying to take back roads and alleys as much as possible, I found myself in a better looked-after part of LA. I hurried down the side of the Pershing Square, grateful it was a weekday and the park was a little less busy than on the weekend.

As a cop car came down the road toward me, I tried to look for somewhere to duck into or a place to hide, but I'd just passed the entrance to a hotel and there wasn't another door or way off for several more yards. I tried to pick up the pace, but the cop looked right at me and then carried on as if I was just a regular tourist.

When the car continued on and the traffic took it out of sight, I felt myself relaxing. If the cops weren't looking for me, then I might just survive this without a problem.

Although I kept an eye out for potential trouble, I relaxed a little and slowed my pace. My leg muscles ached, and my feet were sore. I'd probably already walked a couple of miles that morning since getting off the bus, and I was lugging along a dragon as extra weight right now. If it hadn't been a mythological creature no one knew about, I'd have got it to walk, or fly, but I was supposed to not be drawing attention to myself.

I wasn't far from the market when I saw two familiar-looking black cars. They looked like the ones that had been parked outside my apartment block early that morning. I'd spotted them from the bus as the agents ran back to them. This time I did dip into an alley. Then I counted to sixty and looked out again.

The coast appeared to be clear, the cars gone, swept away onto East 4th Street, but I remained on edge, and tried to walk along just behind another couple, keeping them between me and the cars heading away.

I was just heading across the road to the block the market was in when I saw two men with suits and sunglasses appear to my left, coming out of the park there.

Shitsticks! I hadn't got any cover from that side and it was clear they'd spotted me as they sped up and headed my way. I didn't wait for them to get close or pull guns, but ran as fast as I could toward the market. It was a busy place and I knew there was a good chance I could lose them in there.

I beat them to the building, despite having to run a little slower to stop my bag from bouncing against me. I heard the dragon let out a few noises, clearly not enjoying being jostled around.

I'm just trying to keep you safe, buddy. Settle down and let me hustle. Almost immediately he did so, seeming to hold himself down and against me so the bag had a smaller profile.

Not sure how that had worked when I'd only thought it, I ran onward, making the entrance and darting inside.

I slowed past the security at this end and tried to look less conspicuous, but as soon as I was past them, I hurried on again. I heard yells behind me, the men after me knocking someone over. As I climbed the steps ahead, I dared to glance back, and saw one of them talking to the security while the other helped an old lady gather her cart back up again and everything that had fallen off it.

For a moment our eyes locked. The agent pointed my way but I didn't stick around to find out if they were going to give chase. I needed to get out of here and get lost in the crowd.

As I saw a cap on a stand of hats, I grabbed it and then hurried to duck down the next side route. Tucking in, in front of a tall, well-built man, I grabbed a hair tie out of my pants' pocket and tied my hair up in a messy bun, splaying the loose ends forward. Then I jammed the cap on as quickly as I could.

The label flapped down against the back of my neck, making me jump before I realized what it was. I thrust it up under the cap as well and hoped it would stay there.

Hurrying onward, I ripped off my jacket and shoved it into the bag on top of the dragon. I heard him let out a disgruntled rawrl but I was too busy looking for something else to replace it with.

There was only one stall, and the jackets on it were in plain view of the owner. Still, I was already in trouble. I'd just stolen a hat without thought. What was another item of clothing?

Preparing to sprint again, I grabbed the first jacket that looked like it might fit, yanking it off the stand and knocking the stand over at the same time.

Thankfully, it caused enough ruckus of its own, people's attention was drawn to that as I rushed away with my prize. I slowed for just long enough to pull it on and then I rushed toward the outer door.

As I grew closer, I noticed the security guard on this exit was holding his hand against his earpiece, no doubt trying to listen to something.

Feeling more than a little guilty for what I was doing to the dragon, but knowing it was necessary, I pulled my bag off my front as quickly as I could and slung it on my back. I couldn't disguise it, but I made a mental note to get another one if I got a chance. One that was a little less conspicuous in coloring. And then I matched my speed to the flow of people, pretending to be stuffing money in my pocket and looking down as I went past the guard.

He didn't seem to notice me, looking out for someone with a different look hopefully, and I was soon outside again. Heading for Little Tokyo, where the streets were more narrow and more windy, and there would be plenty of little shops I could hide in, I picked up the pace again.

For now, however, I had lost them. And as soon as I was sure I was in the clear again for a bit, I found a place to stop where no one would notice me, tucking into the opening of another alley. I made sure we were safe and brought my bag back around to the front. Immediately the dragon let out another disgruntled roar.

"Sorry," I said as I pulled my jacket back off his head.

He coughed and looked up at me with narrowed eyes, then snapped at the air a few times.

"You hungry?" I asked. He seemed to nod, but the motion was brief, and I sighed. I hadn't managed to get him any more food, and at this rate, this creature was going to cost me hundreds of dollars a day just to feed him. Where was I going to get that kind of money?

"I'm sorry," I said, not sure what else to say. "I didn't want to let those men catch us. I don't know what they'll do to you. They stopped me from getting more food."

The dragon blinked, almost lazily. I sighed and did the same.

"I'll try to find more food soon, but I think, if you're sticking around, I ought to name you."

I thought for a moment, staring into the distance. What would make a good dragon name?

"Zephyr," I said a moment later. "That name works whether you're male or female. 'Cause I can't tell yet."

The dragon tilted his head to the side a moment, then let out a little growl that sounded like him trying to say the word.

Zephyr.

Less than twenty-four hours after losing my job and having my world turned upside down, I was sitting in an alley with a dragon I owned, or was at least looking after, called Zephyr. My life was officially crazy.

CHAPTER EIGHT

Sighing, I walked the streets again. I'd managed to find a butcher. It looked a little questionable and sold meats that weren't labeled with anything but symbols from another language, but Zephyr had eaten everything without hesitation, and it had been cheaper than finding a butcher or shop in the more westernized parts of LA.

I tried to push away the thought that the reason it had been so cheap was because it had been dog meat or something, but either way, Zephyr had downed it.

"Rawrl," came the little dragon growl from my bag. Immediately, I received a strange look from a passerby, but Zephyr did it again, each time growing louder and higher-pitched as if something was seriously wrong with him.

Hurrying, I ducked into the next alley, grateful it was in shadow and I could head down it a little way.

Zephyr roared again as I swung the bag down to the ground.

"What's up?" I asked, more than a little concerned as I pulled back the top.

The dragon wasn't focused on me, however. As soon as the bag was low to the ground, he hopped out and scurried further up the alley.

"Careful," I said, fear making me panic. What if he ran? Or flew away? What if he was trying to escape? I'd just gotten myself into a world of trouble for this dragon.

I exhaled, relieved, as he squatted his lower end down in the corner and let out a rush of golden liquid.

"Oh," I said. "Oops."

He blinked at me as he also took care of the other type of business. The stink made me wrinkle my nose, but he let out a very happy little noise, sort of like a cross between a roar and a purr before waddling back down the alley toward me.

"Can you fly?" I asked, but Zephyr ignored me, jumping back up onto the bag. This time he didn't tangle his limbs, but as he settled down into his nest again, I noticed there was a little less space than before.

Was the dragon getting bigger? He had eaten plenty so far. Especially for something so small. I had a feeling he was going to grow, though. Like, really grow.

We spent the rest of the day wandering around LA. Twice more I spotted the same men, no doubt on the lookout for me, but both times I managed to duck down an alley or get out of sight before they spotted us.

I also had to buy food a couple more times, as well as water. Three times I had to try to navigate public toilets, but by the time the sun was beginning to sink in the sky, I had a rough plan.

There was no way I could spend the rest of my life walking around LA, and that meant I had to find somewhere to lie low for a bit, and some way of earning some more money. But after a bad night's sleep and all day on my feet, I was shattered.

I had a friend not too far away. Someone I knew would take me in. I just had to get to her house and explain the situation to her. I didn't doubt she'd flip when she saw Zephyr, but I had to get some help looking after him while I figured out how to provide for him and keep the government agents, or whoever they were, away.

Lyra was someone who'd been doing karate with me for months and she could hold her own in a fight as well. I was wary of putting anyone in danger, but she could fight almost as well as I could, and so far the agents hadn't been intending to kill anyone.

I'd waited until it was darker just in case more agents were about, and also because Lyra had a steady day job as an accountant. Something that meant she'd be out all day.

As the sun sank and streetlights came on, I started to walk toward her house, heading back toward the market and the area she lived in. I contemplated getting a bus, but I was still a fair way off the bus route, and I didn't want to head to the metro station on Fifth and risk being cornered in the station. If I were an agent, I'd watch a place like that to see if I was trying to do a runner to another city.

No sooner had I reached the underpass to head to another part of LA than I saw two agents again. Hanging out on the road above, watching. I backed up into the shadows, watching them where they couldn't see me a moment. They were keeping an eye out and talking on radios to someone.

And it didn't look like they planned to go anywhere else any time soon.

Shitsticks, I thought, tired and achy.

My feet hurt and my shoulders felt tense and strange from carrying the dragon all day. I didn't want to have to go the long way around.

Sighing, I backtracked a little, trying to form a new route in my head. I wasn't used to having to navigate by memory anymore. Not in places I'd only visited a few times. That's what smartphones were for. But today I had no choice. I didn't dare put the battery back in my cell phone. Not after they'd hacked it. That meant I had to find my own way by memory.

Another hundred yards and I was ready to try to head over at the next bridge along, but before I could get near it, I spotted a familiar black car. This route was staked out too.

Growling, I backed up for the second time in about ten minutes. I went to head down another block, but I didn't even get halfway down the street when I saw another car creep forward and park.

I turned on the balls of my feet and went back the way I'd come, fear settling like a weight in my stomach. Were they slowly closing a net around me? Had they known I was in this area of LA all along?

The thought wasn't a happy one as the car on the road I'd originally come from also crept forward and paused. More than a little scared, I ducked into the next alley, grateful to find it came out on the next road. I jogged along it, desperate to get ahead of the men and try to find a way around them.

Zephyr lifted his head, appearing disgruntled by my jogging again.

"Don't suppose you want to fly for a bit and help lighten the load?" I asked, but he didn't move the rest of him, merely having a quick look around before he tucked himself back inside again. *I didn't think so.*

As soon as I was out of the alley, I hurried to the right. The car was still where I'd left it, sitting at the curb by the next block down. Knowing I had to try to get out of this place soon, I crossed the road, trying to use someone else as cover, but I must have been noticed because another car appeared further up at the end of the road I was heading toward, and the car behind darted back into traffic and came my way.

Turning yet again, I legged it down the only route that led away from the agents for now, diving into an alley I knew the cars couldn't follow down.

Weaving in and out of the backstreets, I soon found myself in Chinatown, but everywhere I looked, agents were hurrying along or scouring the streets.

I ducked into a small shop selling clothes and prayed they had changing rooms. Someone must have heard me as I spotted the sign within another second. After another few seconds I grabbed a pair of pants, not entirely liking the style but noticing they were my size. I then grabbed another hooded sweatshirt and hurried straight to the changing rooms.

The woman beside them handed me a number and noted what I had. Thankfully that was all the delay and then I was heading into a changing room.

"I've ripped a hole in these pants. Is it okay if I keep

these on if they fit and just take the tag up to the desk to pay?" I called over my shoulder.

"Sure," the woman called back, almost sighing the word. I doubted she cared.

Trying not to panic, I quickly changed, hoping that the agents wouldn't work out where I was and find me before I'd finished changing. The last thing I wanted was to get caught in nothing but my underwear.

The clothes fit well enough, and I pulled the hood up, hiding my hair and ears. Taking a quick glance in the mirror, I saw that I looked different yet again, but I knew my bright bag would give me away. I needed a new one, and it needed to be less obvious.

Heading out of the changing rooms, I asked the woman if they had bags as well. She looked me over as if she wasn't sure what I was doing, but pointed at a small stand.

I quickly grabbed the largest one they had with decent shoulder straps and took it up to the customer desk. It used up most of the rest of my cash, but as soon as I'd paid, I went back to the changing rooms.

"Are you homeless or something?" the woman asked as I tried to go past yet again.

I shook my head, but she moved to block my path.

"I've been homeless before, but I'm not now, although I got fired yesterday." I sighed, not sure how to tell this girl I needed her out of my way.

"So you're, what? On the run?"

"Not exactly. I think I witnessed something I shouldn't have. And I'm just trying to keep a friend safe. I don't want to say any more, but there are a couple of dodgy-looking men following me. I feel like I've been plunged into a movie and I don't know what else to do but change how I look and try to get out of here."

She studied me for a moment, then backed off.

"If they come in, I'll tell them you've gone already and are wearing different clothes."

"Thank you so much!" I smiled as I hurried into another changing room and hastily got the new bag ready.

"Out you hop, Zephyr," I whispered. The dragon lifted up and looked around, and I pointed to the new bag. He tilted his head to the side again, blinking a few times before he jumped onto the bench and regarded the new bag.

Almost shaking with the speed I was moving, I stuffed my old clothes into the bottom and added everything from my old bag, grateful the new one had a couple of bigger side pockets for the snacks and water bottles.

With that done, I tried to make the new one comfy. Once I was sure everything was good enough, I brought it near the dragon and let him climb inside.

He sniffed it a few times, turning in a circle before he settled down, his wings still folded against his back.

"Glad you approve," I added before I bundled up the old bag. For a moment I considered bringing it with me, but I knew I'd never be able to use it again, and it was already showing signs of fraying from all the extra use that day. Better to ditch it.

I lifted the new bag and slung it on my shoulders, feeling the extra weight instantly but grateful for the wider straps that spread the load a little better. Now, I really needed to get out of here and get past those agents.

"I'll find a bin out back for this," the girl on the door said, taking my old bag from me. "Good luck."

"I'm going to need it," I replied as I pulled the hood as far forward as it would come and made my way back to the front of the shop. I couldn't see any more of the suited men, but it was now almost dark, and I had no idea how late it was.

Setting off again and trying to ignore the pain in my feet, I hurried across the street and down another alley. This time I was more cautious as I moved forward. I tried to look calm and leisurely, and I headed in a very different direction, grateful for the people who were coming into the area to get their dinner and helping provide cover.

But an hour later I was still as frustrated, my routes out of Chinatown all blocked and guarded. The men had spread out, for the most part only one on any street or corner, but they were constantly on their radios, and now and then, more pairs showed up and conversed before they set off again in one direction or another.

Just how many agents were out here after me? I had no idea, but it was clear I wasn't going to get out of here while they knew I was in the vicinity. It was as if I needed a distraction.

I wasn't going to get one, however. Given how they'd hacked my phone and wiped the photos of Zephyr's egg, I knew I couldn't risk turning it on again and trying to call someone. I also couldn't stay here.

There was only one option for it. I needed to pick a route out and fight my way past an agent. But the thought of doing so made me tense up even further. I was tired, and it had been a long day. I was also hungry, and from the noises of protest and snapping sounds Zephyr made every now and then, so was he.

I moved around, checking several of the smaller routes out, hoping the agent on one might have gotten complacent and not be paying much attention. Or might be busy doing something else, like checking his phone. They couldn't all be model employees.

Eventually I came across a small route out to the north, over toward the stadium. It was a walkway, and there was just a single agent standing at the far end. I decided to head down it, and shifted my pack to my back so I looked like a normal person. With any luck, I'd look like someone on their way home or to work at the next game.

I walked casually. If my phone hadn't been so old and distinguishable, I'd have pulled that out and tapped away as if it were on, but I didn't dare draw attention to myself by using it in public. Instead, I hummed to myself as if I had earphones in and walked along.

But my whole ruse was over within seconds, a couple of agents appearing to my right before I ever got to the walkway. One of them sported an arm brace and the other had a bruise across his nose and some tape. I gulped. I'd run into these two before, and no amount of different clothing was going to stop them from recognizing me.

They pulled their guns, giving me no choice but to run as fast as I could back the way I'd come. Shots rang out, breaking the glass of the car window up ahead. As I ran past, I saw a dart sticking out of the car's seat cushion.

At least it wasn't bullets, but I nonetheless didn't appreciate being shot at. And there was no way I was going to let them take Zephyr.

Hurling myself around the next corner, I realized there was nowhere else to go but down an almost empty street, or the next road where agents were already running up, no doubt called that way.

Feeling like the net might finally have closed around me, I spotted a kid's playhouse sitting by the trash of the nearest building. I ran to it, hoping I was small enough to slip inside. The door ground to a halt partway open, broken somewhere, but I pushed my pack inside and squeezed in after it.

It was slimy inside, mold and all sorts of dirt on the plastic interior, and it smelled more than a little funky, but I pulled the door shut behind me as best I could and waited in the almost dark of the kid's house.

Trying not to make much noise, I inched around and reached out to check Zephyr was okay. The dragon nuzzled against my hand a moment, but his movements seemed sluggish.

Instantly my heart raced. Had he been hit? I felt along the outside of the bag as I heard the sound of someone running nearby. My fingers found the small round shape of a dart stuck in the side of the bag and through to the soft underbelly of the dragon on that side. One lucky shot. I pulled the dart out, but the drug must have already entered Zephyr's system.

For a moment I feared it was lethal, but Zephyr was soon letting out soft little snoring sounds, and he continued to feel warm to the touch.

Outside more people ran around, clearly looking for me. I didn't move, feeling a sort of safety in the playhouse. Once Zephyr was awake or the agents had given up and backed off, I could consider my next move.

CHAPTER NINE

Several hours had passed before I was sure no more agents were nearby, but Zephyr was still asleep. I stroked him now and then, making sure I rubbed my hand in the same direction as the scales, and hoped that the motion soothed him while he dreamed.

Although I considered staying where I was until morning, or at least for most of the night, I needed to pee, and the confined space was less than ideal. As most of the people who had come to eat in the restaurants here made their way home and the noise in general grew quieter, I dared come out. Maybe the agents would sleep too.

Some of them must have been up as long as I had, and I suspected the two I'd seen last were still going to be up as well. I had a feeling those two wouldn't rest until they'd found me.

Sighing, I stroked Zephyr again.

"Wake up, buddy," I whispered. He stirred but stayed asleep, so I pushed open the door and emerged. I looked around, taking my time before I pulled my bag and Zephyr back out. His weight made me groan again as I lifted him onto my front.

He wriggled against me, letting me know he was still very much alive, but he just snuggled closer and continued sleeping. Sighing, and more than ready to do something similar, I padded back out toward the street, looking both ways before I completely emerged.

At first I didn't think there was anyone there, but then I caught the faintest slither of someone in glasses standing at the far end of the quiet street to my right. I also didn't doubt the walkway to my left would still be guarded. That left me the route straight ahead.

I hurried down that road toward the area where most of the Chinese and other Asian restaurants were, but I hadn't got far before I heard more shouts. I picked up the pace, but everywhere was now shut up and there was nowhere to run.

As I was going past a small alleyway and considering ducking down it, a Chinese man, muscular and tall given his Asian descent, came out, carrying a bin full of rubbish. He pushed open the dumpster and emptied it in as if it was nothing, then looked at me and the bag I had slung to my front.

The smell of stir fry and soy sauce hit my nose, making me slow down.

I glanced over my shoulder, not seeing any agents behind me yet, and then down at my bag. Zephyr was going to be starving when he woke, and I had no idea if the agents would check the restaurant.

"Are you still open?" I asked.

"No," he said in perfect English, although his accent was

definitely foreign. "But if you're the person all those men have been looking for this evening, quick, come inside. I can fix you a bite and let you catch your breath."

I couldn't believe my luck as he backed up and let me head in, but after the day I'd had, I wasn't even going to hesitate.

He led me through the restaurant's kitchens, passing a woman washing a large pot by hand. She didn't turn to look at me although the man spoke in his native language. She grunted in reply as he led me through to the main dining area.

At the first table, he pulled out a chair for me. The tablecloth didn't have any napkins, cutlery or plates laid on it, confirming that he was closed, but he grabbed them and a menu for me.

"Thank you so much," I said as I sank into the chair, my body more than happy to be resting on something so comfortable for a while.

"That's all right. You must have had a difficult day. I'm Minsheng. Relax here for a while and know you're safe."

As I took the weight off my feet, the pain increased for a moment before settling down to a background ache again. I kept Zephyr and the bag on my front, glad the dragon wasn't snoring anymore but not sure what to do with him.

"I can't do everything on the menu since we've cleaned so much up, but I could whip up a noodle dish no problem," he said.

"Something simple is fine," I said, not doing more than glancing. "Just plenty of meat."

The last part was an afterthought, but he nodded and looked at the bag, and his eyes went wide for a moment.

"You want some extra meat for the dragon in there?" he asked.

I blinked, taking a moment to notice my mouth had fallen open. As I shut it, he smiled, then he turned and yelled something toward the kitchen in a language I didn't understand. The woman called something back.

"Must be a young one, recently hatched to fit into a bag that size."

I nodded, not sure how much I should say. What did this man know about dragons?

"Is it yours?" he asked, almost sounding hopeful.

Again I nodded, but I backed up an inch, the chair scraping across the floor.

Suddenly he held up his hands, as if I was aiming a gun at him.

"I'm not going to harm you. It's clear you're on the run. It's just been years since there has been an actual dragon in the country."

"It has?" I asked. "I've never seen one until I found this one."

"Me neither. I've heard all the stories, though." He grabbed a jug of water from the side and a glass before offering me another drink. I shook my head, not sure how much the meal was going to cost as it was.

As he put the drink down, he peeked at the top of the bag, no doubt getting another glimpse.

"Oh, a bronze dragon. Those are rare! They're one of the most powerful. Once they're fully grown, anyway."

"Hungry, too," I replied, not sure what else to say. It was

still a shock that he wasn't in any way surprised or confused by me having a dragon.

"I bet. My mother used to tell me they could eat a person out of house and home. Can't have been easy, keeping him fed on the run."

"Not sure if it's a him or not yet." I looked down again as Zephyr stirred.

"Oh, it's a male. The horns on the head are curved straight back. The females come out to the sides more and have bigger horns, believe it or not."

"Cool."

Any further conversation was interrupted by the arrival of my food. I tucked in, taking the opportunity to focus on something else. Thankfully, the restaurant owner busied himself, popping out of the kitchen now and then to fetch something else to be washed and bringing clean things out for the next day.

The food tasted amazing and made me feel more than a little better, although I ate too fast and had to slow partway through to let the food settle. I was just finishing as Zephyr woke up. Right away, he lifted his head out of the bag and rawrled at me.

Minsheng came out of the kitchen immediately, holding a huge bowl full of chargrilled meats and noodles and veg. It looked like a meal for a person, not a dragon, but Zephyr appeared to approve as the guy set it down on the floor near the bag. The dragon jumped out and landed right beside the bowl. A moment later, he stuffed his face in and started chomping it down even faster than I'd been eating.

I didn't take my eyes off him as Minsheng lingered nearby.

"He's very young. Only a few days old?" he asked me.

"Hatched this morning," I replied, startling myself. Had it still been so little time? I felt like I'd been on the run forever. "And he's already eaten his weight in food several times over. And crapped to go with it."

More than once, I'd had to find him an alley. He'd even done one in the toilet the recent times I'd been. He was learning fast, and he was bright.

"You'll need to teach him to fly soon. The air magic should help with that, though."

"Air magic?" I asked, wondering how this man knew so much and if he was for real. As far as I'd been aware this time yesterday, dragons, magic, and all these sorts of things had been the stuff of fairy tales and myths, not the things that happened in the real world. He was sitting in his own restaurant, acting as if feeding a dragon and discussing his development was normal.

"You haven't been practicing it? Are you elven on your mother's side or your father's?" This time Minsheng looked at me as he spoke, moving so he could see the sides of my head. He then pointed, no doubt noticing the blank expression I gave him.

"Your ears give it away. At least half-elven, I'd say, although you have the eyes and hair of a dragon, so... Silver dragon in there? Or..." He trailed off when I still didn't respond.

"I'm an orphan," I replied. "I was adopted, and no one knows who my parents were."

Minsheng sat down like someone had pushed him, staring at me.

"Are you... You're... Your name. What's your name?"

I blinked, surprised by his sudden strange behavior. He'd seemed creepy before, but this was a new level of odd.

"Your name, please? I must know. Are you her?"

"My adopted parents called me Aella-Faye," I said, but I felt uncomfortable. Zephyr paused his eating, looking at Minsheng and me. I swallowed and wondered why this man was so concerned about me, but on hearing my name, he nodded. It looked like he might cry for a moment, his eyes glistening.

"Then Aella-Faye, please, let me help you. It's clear you need it," he said, the words tumbling out. "I have a safe house and a training room for your dragon and you to train. I will teach you to use the elven magic inside you."

"I'm sorry, but no," I said, getting up, not sure I liked the gleam in his eyes. Immediately, he got up as well. I put my hand out and he didn't move, respecting my boundaries. Maybe I could bluff that I knew some magic to keep him back.

He looked me over, but it was clear he knew I didn't.

"I don't want to hurt you or your dragon," he said. "And I'm sure you're scared. I am what's called a *Shishou*, and I've been waiting most of my life to find my ward—the bonded elf I'm meant to help guide and train. I believe you're her. Please, let me help you."

I shook my head, not wanting to believe it. He'd been obsessed with my dragon, and even now, he looked at him with the same sort of gleam in his eyes. I wasn't going to let him near my dragon. Not when I wasn't ready to protect it.

Zephyr had almost finished eating and drinking, so I opened up the bag again.

"Inside, Zephyr," I said, taking my eyes off Minsheng just long enough to try to get the dragon in. At first, I was worried he wouldn't obey me, but after a single glance at the well-built man, Zephyr climbed back into the bag and settled down.

"How much do I owe you?" I asked as I picked the bag up and put Zephyr firmly on my front.

"No charge," he replied as I hurried back from the table. I wasn't going to argue when I barely had any money left.

"Thank you for the food and the offer," I said. "But I think I should try to get back to my parents now. They might have adopted me, but they'll be worried about me."

It was a lie. They didn't even know where I was. I called them once every few months to let them know I was alive, but that was it. The conversations were never pleasant and never instigated by them, but he didn't need to know that.

"I truly don't want to hurt you. If you change your mind or find yourself struggling, especially to feed Zephyr, then come back anytime. There will always be food here for you both and a place to hide."

I nodded, not sure how sincere he was, but he moved to the door and unlocked it for me. I tried to hide my shock. I hadn't even realized I was locked into the building until then. Ready to hit myself for my naivety and lack of suspicion, I hurried out the door and back into the night.

Within seconds my back, shoulders, and feet protested, but I knew I couldn't stay. I had decided to protect this dragon, and whatever and whoever I was, I couldn't trust a stranger. Not now that I knew dragons were something rare and hidden, not something mythical.

I wasn't about to trust some random stranger in Chinatown, even if he had fed Zephyr and me. Who knew what they might want Zephyr for? Until he was bigger and could fly, I wasn't going to trust anyone with him.

But I knew I couldn't stay out in the night either. I needed sleep and a way to get some more money. As I thought about the latter, I considered phoning my parents. They were wealthy and might bail me out. Not that I'd be able to explain it to them entirely, but they might take pity, hearing that I'd been fired.

Of course, there was as good a chance they wouldn't help. It wasn't like we had a great loving relationship. And I'd have to put my phone back together and turn it on to phone them. It would draw the agents to me again. Of that, I was sure.

No, my best bet was my friend, and then I'd have to find some way of hiding the dragon and me. Given that I was on the run and had already stolen, maybe I could keep doing that. But no sooner had I had the thought than I knew it wouldn't work. Zephyr was going to eat too much. I needed to go somewhere I could get a decent job and keep Zephyr safe.

Somewhere out in the country, maybe. Maybe the agents would find it harder to locate me if I was in another part of the country. Some quiet hick town where there were plenty of cattle and Zephyr could learn to hunt and catch his own dinner.

It was the only decent idea I'd had, so I walked down the street. I still had no idea what time it was, but the streets were almost silent now. If the agents were still out looking for me, they had grown even stealthier because I saw no one obvious as I wandered along.

Maybe they had given up and gone to sleep?

But as I came to the end of the block, I spotted a car ahead that looked all too familiar, parked almost on the corner.

I froze, not sure what to do, but able to see inside the car enough to notice that the agent inside wasn't looking my way. As I crept closer, the agent's head never turned, and I gained an even clearer view.

By the time I was standing right beside the car, I could see the agent was slouched back a little, fast asleep.

Grinning and fighting back the chuckle I wanted to emit, I moved around the car, keeping on the balls of my feet to make less noise. As soon as I was a bit further away, I moved a little faster, just in case he woke up.

Had I just slipped the net? I hoped so because I was exhausted, my body no longer boosted by the adrenaline fear gave me and so much of me hurting.

"Not long now," I whispered to Zephyr, as much to talk to him as to hear my own voice. "Not long, and we'll be resting in a nice warm bed."

CHAPTER TEN

A couple of times I ducked into an alley, noticing people up ahead and not willing to take a chance, but I was still wandering the streets of LA. Every now and then I passed a homeless person curled up in a sleeping bag or wrapped in cardboard to try to keep the chill off. I felt a pang as I remembered how that had felt.

I didn't want to go back, but I knew I was dangerously close.

Twice I'd seen another agent car, or what I thought was one, but only once had it appeared like someone had seen me and responded. I'd sprinted out of the area before anyone had shown up, however.

Now that I was well on the way to my friend's and not that far from my home, I found myself wondering if they were watching my apartment block. Could I stop by and grab another change of clothes and some more cash?

It might make the following day easier, and it felt like the heat had come off a bit during the night. As I glanced down at Zephyr, I saw he had curled up and gone to sleep.

"All right for some," I muttered.

Sighing, I decided to head toward my old place and check if it was safe. It was only a few hundred yards out of my path, and it wasn't as if I was taking a direct route. The agents had positioned their cars well and were making my route wiggle all over the district.

It didn't take me long to head up Seventh, the street occasionally lighting up as a car came along it. Each time I held my breath, examining the shape and imagining another set of agents leaping out and coming after me.

But mostly, they hurt my eyes. I needed sleep. I really needed sleep.

As I got to the corner of my street, I paused, peering out from the side of a building to see if anyone lingered. At first I thought no one was there, but then someone came out of a nearby house, his phone lighting his face as he walked toward me. As he passed a hedge near the apartment, the light showed the outline of a person hiding.

"At least I'm not the only one out in the cold," I said, but it was a blasé way of hiding the disappointment I felt. I just wanted to rest.

I backtracked and took the street the next block over, grateful that it was unwatched, then made my way to my friend's house. I finally came close about half an hour later, aware that my pace had slowed and I had yawned more times in the last hour than what felt like my entire life put together.

Trying not to be too reckless, I paused at the end of her street and checked for danger.

Although I didn't have much contact with Lyra outside of karate, I did speak to her occasionally. I knew the agents would have thought to watch likely alternative places I'd go, but I desperately hoped they'd overlooked this one. We talked more verbally than by text, in the changing rooms before and after lessons, at bus stops, and when we met at social events.

With neither of us using the phone or social media to communicate, it would look like a far less significant friendship than it truly was. Or at least I hoped so. That was why I'd chosen her to bug for a place to stay and not someone else.

Of course, it also helped that she had a reasonable amount of money. Most of my other friends, the few I had, were poor. I couldn't ask them for help like this.

I couldn't see anything or anyone suspicious despite waiting and looking for what felt like an age. When I thought my shoulders really couldn't take the weight of Zephyr and my belongings any longer, I hurried to her apartment door.

With no idea what time of the night it was but suspecting it was late, I winced as I pressed the buzzer to my friend's apartment. *Sorry, Lyra.*

There was no response until I pressed and held it a second time.

"Piss off. It's three in the fucking morning," came Lyra's voice.

"Lyra, it's Aella," I said quickly, hoping she hadn't immediately walked away. "I'm so sorry for waking you. I swear I'm sober and this isn't some kind of prank. Can I come in?"

"There had better be a good explanation for this," she replied before the door clicked and let me open it.

Exhaling my relief, I pulled it open and slipped inside. I'd only been in the building a couple of times, and it took me a moment to get my bearings, but I soon stood outside her door. It was already ajar, a slipper wedging it open.

"Thank you so much, Lyra," I said as I pushed the door open farther and walked in. I shut the door behind me and wandered through the small apartment, heading past the bathroom, through the hallway, then the living room until I found her in the kitchen making a hot drink.

"Sit. Explain," she said, not even looking around.

"My apartment was attacked by some kind of government agents, and I lost my job," I said. She turned, the kettle now on, and fixed me with a look that said, *I don't believe you.*

I sighed and sat down on one of the kitchen chairs, aware she looked more than a little disheveled. She wore a sweatshirt on top of pajamas, and her hair was tied up in a bun, tendrils of it sticking out all over.

"What kind of shit did you get yourself into? Drugs and crap like that don't seem to be your thing."

"No. Not drugs. I think I accidentally exposed a cover-up." I frowned, trying to think of the best way to explain this without showing her Zephyr. I didn't want to get her into trouble, and at the moment, he was still asleep in my bag. Could I keep his presence from her?

"What do you mean, accidentally exposed?" Her tone was clipped as if she wasn't happy with my story. I exhaled and thought of a way I could tell her most of it without actually telling her I had a dragon. The best lies always contained some truth. At least, that was what everyone said, so I decided to start from the beginning and modify my story as I went. Mostly, though, I could leave out the dragon bit.

I told her about the strange man at work. How I'd been fired and then mugged on the way home. The strange building that wasn't officially on the map.

"I saw something I wasn't meant to. And I took photos," I said.

"That egg?" Lyra asked, making it clear she had seen the social media post before it was deleted. "I wondered what happened to those. Why did you take them down again so fast?"

"I didn't," I replied. "The government did. They wiped them from my phone as well."

Lyra's mouth fell open.

"Oh, crap. Oh..."

"I know. They attacked my apartment. Well, sort of raided it early in the morning. I only just managed to get away. Fought them to get out of the building. Broke a nose and dislocated a shoulder. And I've been trying to lose them all day. Hid in Chinatown in a discarded playhouse for a while. In that abandoned mall, too."

"That sounds like hell. Or something out of a spy novel."

I nodded and yawned, the exhaustion catching up with me.

"You want to stay here and lay low for a day or two?" she asked, her voice sounding softer.

"Do you mind?"

"No. Just don't tell me anything, so if they come after me too, I can tell them I know nothing but what was in the missing pictures and pass one of those lie detector tests."

I nodded. I hadn't been planning on telling her anything else, but I was glad she'd picked up on there being more. It meant I didn't have to keep lying. She didn't want to know.

Within ten minutes, I was curled up on her sofa, my bag beside me. Zephyr had slept through everything, and Lyra was back in her own room. Feeling safe finally, I was out like a light.

The sounds of scratching and then hot breath on my face were the first things I knew, followed by a pained-sounding rawrl. I opened my eyes to see Zephyr jumping around the living room, one foot tangled in the strap of the new bag. A moment later he came to me, let out his adorable little roar, and then hurried back to the living room door.

He'd crashed the bag into stuff, knocking over a guitar and some books off the shelves. I groaned, wondering if he needed the toilet but unable to catch him. The stupid dragon was still running around and dragging my bag behind him.

It took me a while, but I managed to get him to stop as he knocked over a set of nested side tables. Being careful not to hurt him or make even more noise, I unwound the bag, then I opened the living room door. He hurried out, his claws skittering and clipping on the hard floor.

I hope Lyra is a deep sleeper, I thought as I hurried to the bathroom and opened the door. Thankfully, Zephyr seemed to recognize the toilet bowl and tried to jump onto it. His balance wasn't great and he toppled off again, clattering and making more noise.

As I scooped him up and put him on the toilet seat, I realized I was also desperate to pee.

Hurry up, little guy.

A moment later, I heard a scream. I whirled around to find Lyra standing in the bathroom doorway, eyes wide, hand over her mouth, pointing at Zephyr.

"Morning," I said, not sure what else to say. There was a small dragon in her bathroom, crapping in her toilet. That was bound to freak anyone out.

"It's a dragon," she said, looking between him and me.

"Yeah, but you asked me not to tell you. He was desperate to take a dump, though. Don't worry, he's already fairly house-trained."

"I can see that," she replied, still rather pale and now clutching the doorframe.

I flushed away the stink as he got down and then looked at her, his head tilted to the side.

"How friendly is it?" Lyra asked, staring back at him.

"I don't think you want to look at him so directly, but Lyra, meet Zephyr. Zephyr, meet Lyra."

"You named it?" She looked to me as if I'd grown an extra head and then back at Zephyr. Appearing to be bored with her and not seeing her as a threat, he looked up at me and rawrled again, snapping his jaws the way he did when he was hungry. Then he made another noise that almost sounded like "food."

"Did he just ask for breakfast?" Lyra backed up a little as he took a step toward her.

"I think so. Got any salami or sausages? Or bacon?" I

asked as I relieved myself as well. Lyra nodded, backing out into the hallway as the dragon started to look around. I was wary about letting him out of my sight and aware he'd already partially trashed her living room, so I followed as soon as I could.

She took her time padding after him, seemingly oblivious to the mess he'd made as he sniffed his way through to the kitchen. He went straight to the fridge and pawed the bottom the way a small dog might when it wanted breakfast.

"You're right about it being house-trained," she said, opening the fridge by leaning a long way over Zephyr. A moment later, she pulled out the bacon. He backed up, his eyes never leaving the packet of meat.

"Does he eat it raw or cooked?" she asked.

"He's had everything cooked so far," I replied, although I had no idea if he could eat it raw. It was possible.

This seemed to help Lyra. She got a pan out and started cooking, focusing on her task. I did the bare minimum to clean myself up and brushed my hair. I kept an eye on Zephyr, but now that he could see someone getting him food and he wasn't desperate for the toilet, he was glancing around the kitchen as he waited to be served,.

By the time I looked a little more decent again and was fixing us all coffee, Lyra had made three plates of food. One was full of meat for Zephyr, and the others held breakfast for each of us.

"You're amazing," I said as we all sat down and started eating.

"Yup, but you're lucky I didn't have to go into work early today." Lyra kept glancing at Zephyr, but she finally appeared to have calmed down and accepted the fact that she had a dragon in the house.

It helped that Zephyr was so small and hadn't tried to do anything like breathe fire yet. But the guy at the restaurant had said something about me teaching Zephyr to fly. I had no idea how I was going to do that, but he looked bigger again that morning, and he had wolfed down his food again. If he could fly, that would be more than useful.

When we'd all eaten, Lyra got back up again.

"Right, I've got to go, but stick around. I'll talk to my brother, and we'll see if we can get you somewhere safer. I assume you're keeping the new pet."

"Of course," I replied. "Although I'm not sure he's a pet."

"Well...whatever. I didn't expect *this* when you said you'd stumbled over a government secret and had found some kind of creature. I expected that they'd been hiding how badly we'd polluted our planet and mutated a fish or something, not actually located a mythological creature. Even in miniature form."

I grinned as Lyra gathered up her belongings, downed the rest of her coffee, and headed toward the door.

"I'll see you when you get back," I said.

"Oh!" she exclaimed, reaching into the pocket of a coat hanging up by the front door. A moment later, she held out a phone to me.

"Here. My old one. It will give me a way to contact you that the government doesn't know is you yet."

"Perfect," I said, grateful to solve that problem. It had felt strange going a whole day without a phone.

With that, she left, leaving Zephyr and me alone in her apartment.

To keep myself busy, I started cleaning up the breakfast mess and setting everything Zephyr had knocked over in the living room right. By the time I was done, he had managed to climb the bookcase in the corner of the room.

I looked at him as he eyed the ground and shuffled a bit. Seemed I wasn't the only one who had decided it was time he learned to fly.

CHAPTER ELEVEN

I had my hands on my hips and was staring at Zephyr. He was standing at the top of the bookcase for the third time and eyeing up the drop, moving back and forth from one foot to the other. It was clear he was scared, and in one sense, I wasn't surprised. He'd fallen off the cabinet twice now and hadn't managed so much as a smidgen of flying.

Each time he'd sort of crash-landed, I'd winced. It looked like it hurt. I was desperate to help him, but I didn't know what to do, and I was fairly sure mother birds just waited as their babies learned to fly the hard way. It wasn't easy, though, and it left me a little bored when he took over twenty minutes of wriggling, bobbing, and shuffling before he finally got up the courage to try again.

Internally, I willed him on. Externally I didn't dare speak in case I distracted him or made him so frustrated he walked away and gave up. The longer it went on, the more worried I was that this might end with broken limbs, or the poor boy might never fly. He looked at me as he gripped the edge with his front claws, still moving back and forth.

"You can do it, Zephyr," I said, feeling like I had permission to provide input. He let out a rawrl, looked at me, and jumped. His little wings unfurled, but not in time to flap before he hit the ground.

Lying on the floor, he flopped his head down and let out a soft, long, tired roar. I went to him and took care not to hurt him as I scooped him into my arms. He sighed and rested his head on my shoulder, nuzzling into me.

I melted, barely daring to breathe or move in case it ended the moment.

"We'll try again," I said a moment later. Not sure what else to do to comfort him, I very gently ran my hand over the scales on his head and down his back. He seemed to shimmy under my hand, pushing up into the stroke.

As I did it again, he sighed once more and let out a deep, throaty noise that might have been a purr. I kept petting him, grateful we were bonding and that he seemed to prefer me to anyone else.

Had we bonded? Was something magical happening between us? It was possible. I wouldn't have believed in magic before two days ago, but now here I was, standing in a friend's living room, cuddling a dragon after it had tried to fly and failed. It wasn't exactly normal times.

I was trying to consider what I wanted to do about the next stage of my life when the spare phone Lyra had given me went off. It vibrated in my pocket until I pulled it out, still cuddling the dragon.

"Hey," Lyra said as soon as I answered. "I have great news. My brother said you could stay with him for a bit. He lives out in the sticks in Nebraska. You'll be fine there."

"That was quick. You sure he won't change his mind

when he learns about Zephyr, though?" I asked. Lyra had reacted well, but she knew me. By the time I got to her brother's, Zephyr would be bigger, and he didn't know me.

"Oh, I told him you had a dragon with you. He didn't believe me at first, of course. Thought I was yanking his chain, but he got there in the end. Told him I'd seen it with my own eyes and that you'd send a photo or something."

I gulped, a weight forming in my stomach as Lyra continued to talk about her brother's reaction and how she'd convinced him. She'd just told her brother I had a dragon. Would the agents trying to track me down have their ears out enough to have noticed that? Were they about to find me because Lyra had spoken about the dragon out loud?

Not every call from every person ever could be monitored. It wasn't possible, but I knew there were keywords. Things people listened out for. Words that triggered monitoring. Was "dragon" one of them?

Feeling more apprehensive as Lyra told me when I could go and how I could get there, I moved over to the windows. Only half-listening to her, I looked outside and tried to surreptitiously check for signs of any agents.

At first there was nothing but the usual traffic, so I gave Lyra my focus again. But a black car soon pulled up, coming down the road. A second was not far behind it.

"Shit," I exclaimed, backing away from the window.

"What?" Lyra said, still on the other end of the phone.

"They're here. They must have traced your call or tapped in or something. They've worked out that I'm here at your house." I grabbed my bag and pulled it open. As

Zephyr jumped down to the floor, I started to shove all my clothes and belongings back into it.

"The agents who want the dragon?" Lyra asked.

"Yes, the people trying to take Zephyr back. You led them straight here."

"What? They can't be there. I don't want my apartment trashed. I'll lose my deposit."

"Then maybe you shouldn't have told your brother there was a dragon in your apartment!" I hung up and chucked the phone on the sofa, not trusting it. Then I held the bag open for Zephyr. He let out a little rawrl and for a moment, acted as if he didn't want to go back inside, but while he couldn't fly, I wasn't going to leave him out of it. Especially as he'd draw lots of attention.

I scooped him up and put him inside before grabbing the bag and slinging it over my back.

He let out another disgruntled roar as I rushed to the door.

Instead of trying to go down the main stairs, I hurried to the back of the building. There was a set of fire escape stairs on the back, the kind that had been installed at a later date to make the building meet newer fire safety regs. I was closer to it than the agents. Hopefully, I could get to the bottom before they arrived.

A window opened onto it, which I pushed up. My arms burned with the sudden exertion, the frame almost sticking several times. It was all I could do to stay calm as I put one leg out the window and onto the metal landing of the escape. The bag and Zephyr caught on the top of the window for a moment and I winced, hoping I hadn't hurt him, before I lowered myself and pulled my other leg out.

As soon as I had my bearings, I dropped the ladder and clambered down to the next floor, repeating the process until I only had one more set to go.

Agents came around the corner, pointing their guns at me. Glancing their way, I carried on. If they were going to shoot at me with tranquilizers, I wasn't going to keep still. Knowing they weren't using real bullets made it easy to act as if there wasn't a weapon aimed at me.

They didn't shoot, coming closer instead. I thanked my lucky stars that they had the sense not to shoot at me while I was climbing down the steps and pushed down the last ladder. For a moment I contemplated going back the way I'd come, but the lead agent was talking into his radio. I knew he was calling for backup and letting them know where I was. If I went back, they'd have someone waiting at the top in no time.

As I got to the bottom, the nearest agent stepped closer.

"Stop," he said, but I shook my head.

"I'm not letting you have the dragon back. He's bonded to me now," I replied and rushed away from him. He shot, but either his aim was off, or he hit my bag again because I didn't feel a sting.

Adrenaline pumped through me, helping me get up to speed and making my heart race. I headed to the corner of the building and ran down a walkway that went out to the street. I didn't doubt there would be more agents there, but I had to get out of the area, and I was in a less familiar part of LA.

As I reached the corner, an agent appeared by my side. Instinctively I put my hands up, expecting him to slam into me. He shot, but both he and the dart seemed to fly back, pushed by an invisible force.

I didn't wait to find out what had happened. The arm I'd put up was tingling like it had been hit. Breaking into a full sprint, I tried to get to the next street before any more agents appeared.

A car pulled up across the end of the street I was hurrying down, two men getting out and dashing my hopes. Glancing behind, I considered turning, but another four agents came up the street. My odds were better continuing, but it was important I didn't get sandwiched between them.

The two ahead pulled their guns and went to shoot me as well, but I didn't slow, instead weaving a little and watching for them to squeeze the triggers.

Hearing myself growl with anger and frustration, I closed the distance between the men ahead and me. At first they looked determined and stern, but they shot several times, each dart missing, until finally one hit me, stinging my stomach as it hit.

A woozy feeling filled my head, but I ran on, stumbling but fighting through it as I plucked the dart out and let it drop to the ground.

All the men lowered their guns and relaxed as if waiting for it to take hold of me.

Despite feeling like someone had stuffed my head full of cotton, I continued to run forward. Reaching the first of the agents, I threw myself at him. Shock made him slow to respond as we both went down.

He tried to grab my wrist as I got up again, but I dug my thumb into the soft flesh between his thumb and forefinger and wrenched myself free. Wobbling a little and having to catch myself on the brick of the house beside me, I got to my feet.

As the second agent lifted his gun again, I automatically smacked at it, sending it flying toward the road. It skittered over the roof of the car before clattering to the asphalt.

The agent growled and lunged toward me, but my body moved instinctively, years of training kicking in even in my woozy state. I felt my head growing even worse, but I managed to thrust out a hand, catching the agent in the chest and making him stumble back.

Not waiting for him to regain his balance or the other agents to catch up, I ran at the car and the open door, using the bottom edge of the open frame to boost and propel my body up and over the top of the car. I didn't get very far before gravity brought me down on it with a bump. I hadn't got as far as I'd hoped, the extra weight of the bag and dragon on my back making this harder, but I could reach the other side of the car. I dug my fingers into the lip of the door on the other side.

Pulling myself across, I used the last of my momentum to swing my legs around and slide off the other side. Again I stumbled, supporting myself on the wing mirror of the car for a second before it broke off in my hands. I threw that at the first agent who appeared, coming through the car rather than over it. Reacting by instinct, he caught it, leaving me to run.

Again I sprinted, my legs wobbly but still moving me. I needed to find a hiding place and soon, since my eyes felt heavy. As soon as I reached the alley on the other side of the street, I ran down it. More shots rang out before I made the corner, but there were no more stings, and I didn't wait to see if Zephyr had been hit.

The alley I'd chosen was little more than a dirt track between the houses, but it soon opened into a paved area, a small road leading back to the main one. It was full of cars and garages. I ran through it, stumbling into a car I didn't give a wide enough berth as more of the tranquilizer pumped around my body.

I couldn't remember ever feeling so sleepy, but a grunt from Zephyr reminded me that I had to get him safe. Somehow I had to keep going.

The small road led to another bubble of car parking and garages, but I was still fifty yards from it when a car turned into the road ahead. At first I thought it was another agent, but it was the wrong color, and it waited for me to get out of the way and hurry into the open parking lot behind it.

As I came around the corner, I saw that one of the garages had been left open slightly, a car close enough to it that it couldn't open fully. I darted straight for it, the car that had waited for me now heading down the road and blocking the agents from following for a moment.

I heard them yelling as if they were trying to get the car to back up, but I was already hunkering down, pulling my bag off my back. A moment later, I was pushing it into the garage ahead of me.

After a brief pause, I squeezed through after it, finding the garage full of boxes, with barely enough space for me. Despite that and the darkness within, I turned and pulled the garage door closed behind me, taking care to not draw attention to myself.

It rattled a little but not too much, and then I was in the

dark, a small rim of light underneath and up one side letting me know it wasn't a perfect fit. My whole body sagged on the floor, Zephyr close by in the bag.

Sleep continued to try to claim me, but I did my best to focus on staying awake. Somehow I kept the strong desire to close my eyes at bay.

I heard the sound of approaching feet outside, others running, and cars, but no one came toward me. It went quiet for a little while until Zephyr let out a small rawrl.

Reaching for the bag, I felt at the opening and found his head. He rested it against my palm, seemingly satisfied to know I was there. As I calmed, I let my eyes slip, but the desire to fall into a deep sleep was beginning to fade, and my head felt a little clearer.

Whatever was in those tranquilizers, it hadn't been a strong enough dose, at least not for me. I worried that they'd realize it, but for now, I'd gotten away again.

Despite being safe, I sighed. I was back to having no plan whatsoever.

CHAPTER TWELVE

I stayed in the garage for a while, letting my head clear. I eventually remembered I had several lights in my bag, the Statue of Liberty becoming my beacon once again as I got my bearings. Zephyr hopped out as I lit up our surroundings.

The garage proved to only have several stacks of boxes at the front of it, and I managed to move around the space, going deeper and finding all sorts of other items. From the dust and stacked nature of the boxes, I was pretty sure the garage was used as storage more than anything else. Out of curiosity, I took a good look around.

There wasn't a lot that was useful, although I was tempted by the small camping stove and gas canister I found at the back, along with a tent. I did take the small saucepan and the utensils, however, as well as the iodine drops I found for purifying water and more butane for the lighter I'd taken.

It would serve as everything I needed to cook if I was out in the wilderness. I could make a fire if need be, and as long as I had food, I'd be okay. With any luck, as Zephyr grew, he would be able to hunt and help me in that regard, but I couldn't be sure. I did know I couldn't stay in a city being watched.

I paused for a moment in front of the small tent. It was packed in a bag and hung by a cord. Could I take that as well? I had a feeling using public transport wasn't going to be a good idea. Could I hike into the wilderness with Zephyr and live out in the middle of nowhere alone?

Feeling impulsive, and not sure I had a better idea, I took it.

As soon as I had all my new gear in my bag or fastened to the outside, I surveyed it. Zephyr was definitely growing, but I was also gaining more stuff. Nowhere in the garage was there a blanket or a sleeping bag, which I'd also need, and until Zephyr could fly and hunt reliably, I was going to have to buy food. That meant I needed more money.

I had a little more stowed back at my apartment. Well, had. There was no way to know if it was still there, and I didn't want to run into the agents again, not yet. My body was still a little slow, and I didn't know whether I could take another hit with a dart and not end up snoring.

For now, I considered heading back to the abandoned mall or staying where I was for a bit longer. I'd have been in favor of the latter, but Zephyr went to the door and lifted a paw to push at it, then he looked back at me.

No doubt he was hungry, needed to crap again, or both.

"All right, Zephyr," I said. "Looks like we're braving the outside world again."

Letting him stay out of the bag for now, and more than

a little grateful that it would make it lighter, I pulled the string to release the garage door and pushed it upwards. The light almost blinded me at first, but I took a moment to adjust.

As I did, I realized Zephyr had already darted out. Panic filled me, making me rush to crawl back out as well.

The dragon hadn't been out of my sight since I'd found him and he'd hatched. Even when I'd slept, I'd gone to sleep with one hand on him and woken with him in the same room as me.

But when I got outside, I found him peeing against the front wheel of a nearby car. He then shuffled farther round and did the rest of his business. The smell was enough to take my fear and turn it into disgust. This was why I'd never had a pet. They were revolting, and cleaning up poop was not something I ever wanted to do.

Thankfully, I had no way of cleaning up Zephyr's. Although I felt a little guilty, I couldn't stop him from going when he needed to. At least most of the time, I'd managed to get him to a toilet.

Once he was done, he scurried up to me but walked along at my side, his tail swishing back and forth. A couple of times he stretched out his wings, but he didn't try to fly. While we were in an area of LA that wasn't very busy and mostly residential, I let him walk. I couldn't keep him in my bag forever, and I suspected he wouldn't fit anymore either.

I kept to the back streets and alleys and looked out for more agents. Twice we went across a busy road, but I waited until there were no cars coming toward us before we hurried across. Zephyr already seemed to understand that you didn't tangle with cars and needed to be careful. He stuck by my side and waited for me to begin crossing before he'd go anywhere near the street.

Down an overgrown alley, he suddenly stopped and sniffed the air. For a moment I considered picking him up, thinking he'd grown tired. Instead, he darted through a bush into a garden and under the deck via a broken section and some steps. I gasped and called his name in a whispered shout.

There was no response, but I heard the sounds of scuffling and some high-pitched squeaking. The fourth or fifth screech was cut off, then there were a few more scrabbles. Zephyr reappeared, backing up as he wriggled out.

I gasped as he pulled a large rat out with him, the creature dead in his jaws. Still sitting in the middle of a garden I couldn't get into, he tore the rat into three chunks and ate each one, leaving nothing but the tail.

Swallowing and feeling a lot less ready for lunch, I could only watch with a sick sort of fascination. My dragon was gross, but at least he knew how to hunt. Before I could call him over, he darted in again, and there were more scuffles and noises. I heard him rawrl and growl, then more squeaks.

Looking both ways down the alley, I made sure no one else could see what was happening and concentrated on the house. There were no signs of movement inside, but that didn't mean no one was home.

Zephyr soon reversed out again, though, with a slightly smaller rat in his mouth. This one wasn't dead, but it seemed to be in a stunned state.

It was dead before it hit the ground again, Zephyr's jaws chomping down on it.

This time I looked away while he ate, once again keeping lookout. He ate a bit slower but left the tail again. As soon as he was done, he came toward me, squeezing back through the hole in the fence and the bush with a little more effort.

Then he trotted down the alley as if nothing had happened or changed and stopping to eat a few rats was a normal part of life.

"That answers my question about whether you'll know how to hunt," I said. It didn't mean he'd catch food for me, but it at least meant I could take him into the country and be fairly confident he'd keep himself alive.

It was the next-best plan I could think of—find some remote place where there was plenty to hunt. See some of the country I'd grown up in. Keep moving, and give Zephyr time to grow large enough that government agents weren't going to be able to keep him a secret any longer.

The plan wasn't foolproof, but it was better than no plan. It was clear I couldn't trust others. Lyra had meant well, but these agents were using technology to find me— cameras, social media, phone tracking, and who knew what else. I needed to get away from all of it.

I still needed money, however, and I had no idea where I was going to get that.

As we reached the end of the alley, I noticed there wasn't one on the other side of the road. We needed to head along a busy street for a bit, and that meant I would have to hide Zephyr again.

Putting the bag down on the ground, I motioned for

him to get into it once more. He seemed to sigh but came closer.

"I know, it's not ideal. But until you can fly, this is the safest way for us to travel. I'm going to find us somewhere we don't have to run so often, okay?"

Zephyr nodded before climbing into the bag. He was definitely growing, and his head poked out of the top of the bag even once he had sat down and curled up. Of course, it didn't help that there was more in the bag along with him, but it was stuff we needed.

I groaned as I lifted the bag again. Zephyr was also heavier, and my arm and shoulder muscles protested at taking the extra strain. I definitely needed a more permanent solution and soon.

Hurrying toward the busier part of town, the shops and banks, I wondered if there was a way I could get some cash. I had been willing to take abandoned items like the lighter and statues, and in my haste to get away, I'd stolen a coat and a cap from bustling stalls. Finally, I'd taken the camping equipment from an unlocked garage. Despite all that, taking large sums of money from someone didn't feel right. Everything else had been one of many or not currently needed. It wasn't taking money someone might need for rent or food or bills.

But I needed money to buy food at least. I didn't want to have to keep stealing that either. It just made it more likely I'd get caught or noticed, and the idea was to be less conspicuous for a while.

I knew Lyra would lend me a little, but I'd gotten her in enough trouble. I didn't doubt those agents would ransack her apartment and maybe even take her in for questioning.

I didn't think they'd hurt her. They weren't trying to do more than tranq me, and I was the main threat in this situation.

That left me with only one source of funds I could think of—my parents. Would they give me money if I told them I was having some trouble and needed it? Could I phone them?

As I ducked down the next alley and relaxed a little, I thought about how I'd do it. I couldn't talk to them for long, and I'd need to put the battery back in my phone. The agents had tracked Lyra's calls, so I didn't doubt that if I powered up my cell again, they would be able to track it. I would also need to get to a bank and take my cash out, assuming my parents gave me any.

And then I'd need to get away yet another time from the inevitable attention all this would draw. I would need somewhere to hide again. Somewhere to make it hard to find me after I'd made my location known.

The old mall was out of the question. It only had one way in or out, and I'd been there before. I wasn't going to take the risk and assume they didn't know I'd gone there. Not to mention that I didn't think Zephyr would fit under the shutter of the shop I'd chosen anymore.

That meant I had to think of a new place to hide. Despite the owner's offer, I also didn't think I could hide in the restaurant in Chinatown. I didn't know the man very well, and he had shown a lot of interest in Zephyr. If he was genuinely trustworthy and caring, I didn't want to get him into trouble, and if he was up to something, I didn't want the risk of not getting away from him.

It left one place. Only one place I could think of where I could hide and stood a chance of getting away.

Elysian Park.

There were trees and all sorts of shrubs in there, and the paths and roads were wiggly at best. Of course, there was also a chance I'd get lost, but I was willing to take that chance.

Heading toward it, I kept my eyes peeled for a bank, trying to think of the closest place I could get cash wired to it. There was only one I knew of for sure. I hadn't been to Dodger Stadium, so I didn't know what was around there, but I didn't want to leave this to chance. I had to phone my parents and get the cash at the same time.

It took me a while to travel to where I wanted to go. Now and then, I saw a car that might have agents inside. The sleek black shape was becoming familiar, but I managed to duck inside a shop or down an alley just in time, and yard by yard, I made my way toward Chinatown and Dodger Stadium.

Along the way, I spent the last of my cash on more water and snacks, mostly for me. It was past lunchtime by the time I was even close to Chinatown, and Zephyr had eaten a couple of rats since breakfast.

I munched, letting him have some of the crumbs, grateful once again that it was the middle of a workday and the city was quieter than it would be later that evening. With his head poking out of the top of the bag I carried, he wasn't as well hidden. Thankfully, no one seemed to notice, although I suspected that if they did, they would assume I was carrying around a stuffed toy for some reason.

The ache in my body grew and the pains in my feet came back, fresh blisters no doubt forming over the old. It made me feel miserable, but it wasn't the first time I'd spent all day on my feet. I'd pull through this. I just had to get out of town.

CHAPTER THIRTEEN

Standing by the bank I'd need to use, I slipped my purse and bank card out of my bag and made sure Zephyr was as hidden as I could get him. I didn't want this to go wrong or take any longer than necessary.

Taking several deep breaths, I held the battery and my phone. This was it. Now or never. I quickly shoved the battery in and put the back on, then I pressed and held the power button.

As soon as the phone came on, I started walking away from the bank and the stadium. If the agents could track my phone, I wanted them to think I was moving in another direction entirely. The screen came on, and I navigated to the contacts. After glancing around, I found my parents' number and called them.

The phone rang several times, and a fear that they might not be there to answer filled my head. They had lives, and I was phoning during a workday. Who knew what they were up to and if they'd even answer?

"Pick up," I said under my breath, my heart begin to

race. I didn't want to be on the call any longer than necessary. I didn't doubt that the agents after me were already picking up on this call.

I kept walking, although not at the same speed, so I could listen and keep an eye on the surroundings. Some of Chinatown wasn't awake yet, the restaurants only opening for dinner, but the rest of the shops and eateries were letting people in.

On the ninth or tenth ring, someone picked up, and relief instantly flooded through me. One hurdle surmounted. Now I just needed to figure out how to tell them I was screwed but not mention the dragon I was protecting.

"Hello?" my mother said, her voice clear but businesslike.

"Hi, Mom," I said. "I'm sorry to just call out of the blue, but I really need some help."

"This is very out of the blue, Aella-Faye," she replied, ignoring the plea I'd just made. I clenched a fist, beginning to feel angry at the tone she'd used.

"I lost my job," I said. "I got fired because some jackass grabbed me and then blamed me when I defended myself."

"And you want me to do something about it?" Her voice went icy-cold, like she expected something so low of me.

"No. I don't want the job back, but I need a month's rent," I replied. It wasn't true. I never planned on going back to the apartment, but she didn't need to know that, and neither did the agents I was sure would be listening in.

"Right. So you run off to God knows where, don't call, barely even bother to ask how we're doing, and the second your little life hits a rocky patch, you phone asking for money?"

"I know it's not great of me, Mom, but I don't want to end up on the streets. I made a single mistake, okay? Do you think I should have let myself get groped at work?"

My mom fell silent, either lost for words or getting angrier. I felt a little bad. I was guilt-tripping her into giving me money, but she was my parent. She'd decided to adopt me. And at some point I'd pay her back, along with everyone else who'd helped me. I was going to make a list as soon as I wasn't running so much. Everyone would get something back for what I'd needed.

"How much is your rent?" she asked, sounding a little calmer, almost resigned.

I exhaled and closed my eyes for a moment, knowing this was the best-case scenario I could hope for: rugged acceptance, disapproving coldness, but a little bit of cash. But what to say? I'd considered the amount to ask for, but for a moment, I couldn't say any of them.

"Seven hundred," I said a moment later. It was a slight lie. My rent was only a little over six hundred a month, but I lived in a pretty rundown part of LA. If I asked for too little, Mom might pick up on it and know something was up.

"I can lend you eight hundred so you can eat for the next little while too. But I'm lending it to you, Aella-Faye. I expect you to pay back every last cent." She crunched down on the last word, and I could imagine the look on her face as she said it, and the way her jaw had snapped shut, and the whiteness of her knuckles as she gripped the phone and tried not to show her anger.

"Thank you. That would be great. I'll pay it all back as soon as I have another job. I'm already out looking for one," I replied.

"I should hope so. What are your bank details?"

I froze for a moment, not sure I should disclose them while I was being listened in on but having no other way to give them to my mom. I read them out as quickly as I could, groaning on the inside when Mom insisted on reading them back to me.

"Thank you," I said as she informed me she'd sent me eight hundred dollars, relief flushing through me. "I've got to go. I've got an interview in only a few minutes."

"Well, that's something, at least. I hope you're well-dressed and you stay polite."

"I'll do my best," I replied.

"Good." Mom's voice softened. "Let me know how it goes."

"Sure, Mom," I replied, knowing it was a lie but appreciating the response. I couldn't afford to let her know anything, not until I was safe and sound somewhere else. For now, it would have to do.

I hung up and pulled the battery back out again, killing the phone.

Shoving it into the bag, I rushed toward the bank I'd picked out. I had to get there as soon as possible and get the money out before agents showed up and tried to take me somewhere else.

While I hurried along, I tried not to panic or look like I was rushing more than necessary, opting for a fast walk. It wasn't easy. It felt like the few hundred yards I'd walked in the other direction while on the phone had opened up a gully between the bank and me, a gap so wide it would take a lifetime to cross again.

Eventually, I reached the bank's door. Glancing left and right to see if there was any sign of trouble, I ducked inside and headed for the line to see a bank teller.

The amount I wanted couldn't be withdrawn in cash any other way than through a face-to-face transaction, so I had no choice but to wait. Every few seconds I glanced at the door, grateful I could do so without turning my head and looking suspicious. No one came through, but it didn't make me feel any more relaxed.

When I reached the counter and the clerk looked at me, I requested to withdraw everything I could without closing the account, holding up the bank card he'd want to see.

He raised his eyebrows at me, but the expression was brief and he went back to his task. Only when he was counting out the cash did he notice the head poking out of my bag.

"Is there a strange dog in there?" he asked, stopping partway through.

"No," I replied with a forced chuckle. "It's a stuffed toy for my niece for her birthday."

Once again the lie rolled off my tongue, and I thanked the life I'd led for making me much more skilled at lying than I ought to be.

"Oh... Well, I hope she likes it," he said before continuing to count my cash. I smiled and thanked him as he handed it over. With all the money I'd had and everything my mom had sent, he gave me just over a thousand. I stepped away from the counter to a more private space off to one side and stuffed it deep down into my bag.

Feeling a little better for having managed that, I hurried toward the door. I didn't get outside before someone walked past in the getup—a black suit and sunglasses—as the other agents I'd seen. I hung back, watching them from behind as they walked away from the stadium. Hopefully, that meant the route I wanted to take would be clear, but I waited a moment longer.

Taking several deep breaths to try to calm down, I headed out of the bank and up the street, not looking back at the agent as if everything was fine.

I couldn't see anyone else, although that didn't mean they weren't lingering down alleys or on walkways. But it was now or never. I had to get out of LA, and at least now I had the cash. I just needed to get a sleeping bag and some food and start my hike.

But I'd only gone a hundred yards or so up the street when I heard a yell behind me. I turned to see two agents, one of them pointing my way. Not waiting for any more to appear or see if they pulled a gun, I ran.

The few people on the streets got out of my way, Zephyr letting out a low growl like a dog, probably at being shaken up so much again. He was still strapped to my front, which made it harder to move, but I didn't have time to swap him around, and didn't think he'd be pleased if I tried to do that at high speed.

Instead, I sprinted away, searching my memories and trying to remember the best route to Elysian Park.

I hurtled out the end of a street and onto a walkway over the freeway. This time there was no agent lingering at the other end, so I started to run across, jogging rather than sprinting when there were other people around. I didn't want to draw too much attention to myself or use up all my energy right away. I still had a long way to run.

Already my breath came in panting gasps, the adrenaline coursing through me, making me feel even more fear. Would they shoot at me again? Or were there too many people around for them to risk something like that?

As I reached the end of the walkway, coming out on a road by the stadium, I dared glance behind. Four agents were now pursuing me, but none of them carried guns where I could see them. It was something, at least.

I had just reached the corner of a building when another agent appeared.

Unable to slow or turn out of his path, I barreled into him, and we tumbled into the street. He grabbed at my wrist as I rolled so Zephyr wouldn't get squashed. His vise-like grip clamped down, making me gasp at the pain and let out an indignant growl of my own.

This seemed to attract Zephyr's attention. Still strapped to my chest and between the agent on the asphalt and me, he was in the perfect position to reach out and bite.

He got the agent's forearm, making him let go of me in a hurry. I pushed up from the ground and seized the opportunity to get away.

No sooner was I on my feet and sprinting away again than the agent leaped up as well.

Hoping I was faster, I kept running, aiming for the stadium and the green trees I could see to one side of it. I needed that cover. Needed somewhere to hide for a while and lose the agents on my track.

But the agent with me wasn't going to be discouraged so easily. He reached out for me again, running faster than

I could after so much time spent walking and running in the last forty-eight hours. I tried to duck to one side, but he was almost as quick and managed to snag the bag's strap.

I felt like I'd been throttled or caught in nasty whiplash, the top half of me slowing so suddenly it flicked my feet out from under me. I let out a yelp as the agent reached a hand around, holding me up by the strap and trying to get me into a lock.

Zephyr seemed to sense my distress and burst out of the top of the bag, pulling himself up my torso until his head was above my shoulder. I fought to get my legs under me again at the same time and bring an arm of my own up to block the agent's attempted grip.

As Zephyr roared and seemed to exhale over my shoulder, the agent gasped, and within seconds he went solid like he'd been frozen.

I slid out of his grasp, having to yank on the bag strap to pull it out of his hand. It toppled him over, and he landed in almost the same position. I could see his eyes moving in his face and he still appeared to be breathing, but his limbs and torso wouldn't move.

Had Zephyr just hit the guy with some kind of paralyzing breath?

There was a slight cloud of vapor in the air where the agent had been standing, but I didn't wait around to find out if it had been caused by my dragon. Instead, I hurried off, letting the creature ride on my shoulder for now. I could only hope he wouldn't scare too many people while he was there.

At this time of day, there wasn't a game on at the stadium, so the parking lot and nearby streets were deserted. I skirted around the edge of it, hearing more commotion behind me and aware that more agents were coming. None of the others appeared to be slowed by their fallen comrade.

As I sprinted into another alley, close to the park at last, shots rang out, something pinging off a rail only inches from me.

Great. More tranq darts. Just what I need. But up ahead, I could see my destination—the edge of the park. Just a bit farther.

CHAPTER FOURTEEN

As I made it to the end of the alley, I heard rather than felt more shots, and I desperately hoped that nothing had hit my dragon or me. Unlike the previous two times I'd been running from the agents while they were shooting, my pack was on my front, and that meant nothing was covering my back and protecting it from an attack.

On top of that, Zephyr was on my shoulder. If he was hit and fell asleep, I'd be forced to carry him in my arms. There wouldn't be time to wrestle his unconscious body back into my bag. He needed to fold up too neatly for me to just stuff him in.

Desperate for somewhere to hide that wasn't too obvious, I burst out onto one of the main paths through the park. People immediately spotted me and the dragon on my shoulder. Their eyes went wide and one woman even pointed, trying to get the attention of the guy with her.

I didn't stop running, having no idea what they all must be thinking. I didn't have time to be careful.

But there was nowhere good to hide. Not only were

there too many people, but the agents were gaining on me, and the commotion Zephyr was causing was making it obvious which way I'd gone.

Taking what looked like a smaller path to the right, deeper into the trees, I hoped to find somewhere quiete, somewhere I could get off a path entirely perhaps, but immediately a woman screamed and hastily started doing up her top again, she and an over-amorous lover pulling away from each other.

I didn't waste my breath apologizing when they'd picked such a public place to make out but hurried down the path.

I hadn't gotten much farther before agents appeared ahead of me as well, talking on radios as they spotted me.

Shitsticks.

Once more I ran to the right, hurling myself through a gap in the trees as I felt Zephyr wobble on my shoulder. I flung an arm up to steady him, but it made running harder, and I missed seeing a low-hanging branch on that side. I ducked it just in time, wobbling as I ran.

And came out into a small clearing.

Not what I wanted.

I needed dense, dark trees. Somewhere I could shelter and get lost while I found a way past these agents.

More men came up behind me, and Zephyr let out a whoosh and a roar again from my shoulder. This time I whirled and stepped back in time to see an agent inhale the cloud of gas Zephyr had created.

The agent was soon paralyzed, the same way the earlier one had been. I shoved him into the path of another agent and knocked them both over. Then I set off again in the other direction.

I tried to get across the clearing, but more agents appeared ahead, the pair I'd hurt among them. Growling my frustration, I ground to a halt and tried to run to the left.

More shots rang out, and this time something hit Zephyr. He let out a pitiful rawrl, and I had to catch him. I cradled him to my chest, trying to rest him on the bag and at least get some of him into it.

I stumbled as I caught my foot on a tree root and almost tumbled us both to the ground. Thankfully I didn't overbalance, but it slowed me, and once again the agents shot. I felt a sting on the back of my neck.

Reaching up, I found the dart and yanked it out, then threw it away as I ran. With the ground uneven and the sedative rushing to my head, I almost stumbled again, and my grip on Zephyr slipped.

It was no good. I needed to stop and get him into the pack. I couldn't let them take him.

I rushed past a tree and grabbed a branch to help myself turn rapidly. Nestled against the trunk, I used both hands to pull open the bag and ease him inside. I felt my eyelids fighting my intentions, closing on me as my limbs grew heavier. I gritted my teeth and tried to will myself to focus on Zephyr.

He was limp enough it wasn't hard to curl his back half in, but the agents were close before I could get his neck and head inside. Pulling the zippers up to help hold him in place, I darted out from behind the tree to smack an agent in the stomach with my outthrust hand.

It was more by luck than judgment, but the agent went down. I tried to turn and hurry away again, but my legs were slow to obey and I tripped over myself, only just catching my body before both I and the bag would have slammed into the ground.

By the time I had scurried back to my feet, two more agents had rushed up. They shot toward me again, not trying to close the distance, but I was already moving. Rushing on.

One dart went wide, and the other whizzed by my ear. I flinched to one side and mistimed my move. The agent sidestepped and tripped me with his foot. I turned as I fell, landing on my side with an oof and a flare of pain. I was going to have one heck of a bruise.

Again they shot, and this time a dart hit me in the side. Another rush of sedative hit my body, and the desire to sleep grew overwhelming. My senses seemed to blur as I fought to focus and protect my dragon, the whole world becoming a strange dreamlike fuzz of sounds and colors.

I couldn't let them get Zephyr. I just couldn't.

By biting my lip, I managed to bring more clarity to my vision and regain some crispness to my hearing, but my body still refused to obey me and lift me up and away from danger.

An agent stepped closer, his gaze locked on my face, his gun pointed right at me.

"Target apprehended," someone nearby said. "Taken enough tranqs to put out an elephant."

I blinked a few times, my eyes slower than I'd like as the second agent appeared in my line of sight. He clipped a radio back onto his belt before lifting his gun as well.

"Looks like even two isn't enough to put her under properly. She's still trying to fight it," I heard him say, confirming his was the voice I'd heard earlier, but as my eyes closed on me again, I thought two had been more than enough.

Again I bit down on my own lip, panic still coursing through me enough to keep me from giving up.

My eyes opened as the agent pointed his dart gun at me. There was nothing I could do. He was going to add a third, and I knew I couldn't fight that much of the sedative. I'd lost.

A shot rang out, but I felt no sting. My eyes drooping, I could just make out the silhouette of the agent as he fell. The first agent turned but something or someone shot him as well, a dart appearing in his chest.

Once more I bit my lip, tasting blood this time. I fought to push myself up, but my limbs were like jelly. I soon sank back, helpless to do anything but watch for a while.

Someone familiar walked into view, one of the agents' guns in his hands. He threw it to the ground and came over to me. As his face came close, my vision cleared enough to remember who he was. Minsheng, from the Chinese restaurant the day before. What was he doing with a dart gun in the middle of Elysian Park?

I didn't know, and I couldn't get my mouth to work to ask him.

"Aella?" he called. "Stay with me. You need to keep awake. More agents will be here soon. Your elven blood will clear it out of your system faster and fight it harder for you, but you have to stay awake."

I tried to nod, tried to tell him I was already doing

everything I could, but I was so tired, and my body felt so heavy. I think he frowned at me, but his face blurred as my eyes tried to close again. I had to hurt myself to cause more adrenaline to rush through my veins and help me stay awake.

When I looked at him again, I saw someone wriggling behind. I fixed my eyes on the movement, seeing the agent do something with a syringe. I grunted and tried to point, my arm only lifting a little before the exertion was too much.

It drew his attention to the danger, however, and I saw him dive for the agent. They wrestled, becoming a blur as Minsheng grabbed at something and the two rolled.

Within seconds they were on their feet, fighting. I watched them dance around each other, chunks of time missing and the rest swirling as I struggled to take it in.

There was a loud noise that made me jolt, flinging my eyelids open. I hadn't realized they were closing on me once more. The agent was down on the ground again, arms out like something had put him there forcefully. The restaurant owner was on his hands and knees, pulling at something.

He came over to me again, growing clearer, but it was too much. I was tired, and my eyes just wouldn't stay open. A moment later, I felt a sharp sting on my arm.

My eyes flew open as my heart began to race.

"Adrenaline," he said. "The agents were all carrying shots. It'll keep you awake for now, but you're going to crash in a bit."

I nodded as he helped me to my feet. As the radios crackled and more agents came running, I used my better control over my body to check that Zephyr was okay and arrange him better in the bag.

"Thank you," I said, realizing Minsheng had rescued me.

"I told you I was here to help you. Will you trust me now?" he asked as he grabbed another dart gun and shot at a far-off agent. He missed, but it made the agent recoil.

"Right now, I trust you more than them." I looked at him, not sure how we were going to get out of this mess, but he was calm, and I was far clearer-headed than I had been since the first time the agents had shot me that morning.

"That will do for now," he replied, shooting again. "Come on, I've got transport this way."

I nodded, liking the idea of not having to walk or run again after all the events of the last few days. I liked the idea of getting away even better.

Minsheng ran to the left and I followed, hoping neither of us would get shot at anymore. I had no idea what would happen if I took another dart after the dose of adrenaline, and I didn't want to know how easily Minsheng might succumb.

Thankfully, for a man so large, he could run fast. He seemed to suck in oxygen as if his lungs were enormous. I could keep up but only just, and I was soon panting beside him.

The agents were faster still, however, and the shooting continued, thankfully going wide as we wove around trees and bushes. Now and then, I heard the commotion of others as they tried to get out of our way, but I was forced to concentrate on the path ahead of me, needing to duck under branches and swerve around sudden obstacles.

I went to go left of a bush that Minsheng went right around, but he grabbed my arm and tugged me to the right.

"Not that way," he said. I was about to ask why when the agent closest to us let me know. He ran left, taking the path I'd been intending to take, and he must have set off some kind of trap. He let out a yelp as something fell on top of him. A net, it seemed.

I glanced back and grinned as the muscular man toppled over, entangled and making it worse with his own struggles.

"Did you put that there or them?" I asked.

"A friend of mine did," Minsheng replied. I wanted to ask what friend, but I didn't get a chance to utter that question either. Another pair of agents appeared in front of us.

"Now would be a great time to use some of that air magic," my rescuer said.

"What air magic?" I asked, wondering if he was talking to me. The agents didn't seem to understand either and lifted their guns.

Minsheng sighed and pulled the gun he had as well, intending to shoot. I dodged to the side as they tried to shoot at Zephyr and me again, grateful when I only felt the pain of catching the edge of the bush now shielding me and not the sting of a dart. As the nearest agent came closer, trying to get around the obstacle to shoot me, I sprang out of the other side.

When Minsheng's gun clicked instead of firing to show it was empty, he threw it at the other agent as I ran forward.

The agent ahead of me tried to fire as well, but his gun was also out of ammo. I threw a punch at him and he blocked it, making it clear he had some hand-to-hand combat training, but I was far faster than most. I followed the first punch with a series of raps, finding that the bag on my chest hampered my attacks only slightly.

Having my dragon in front seemed to confuse my opponent. He blocked and defended himself as best he could, but he didn't throw any punches of his own. It gave me a huge advantage, and I used it. Pressing each attack, I tried to find the opening I needed. He soon gave it to me, hesitating as I feinted a few times.

I swept his front leg out from under him at the same time I caught the top of his arm with my hand. When I spun him slightly, he went over. Instead of landing on the ground and making it so I could deliver a knockout blow, he cracked his head on the tree trunk behind. I winced for him as he slid down into a sprawled sort of sitting position, unconscious.

Glancing over at Minsheng, I saw him dancing around with the other agent, neither seeming to want to throw the first punch. I rolled my eyes and was going to wade in until I saw the pistol my attacker had been carrying. Did they have more ammo?

I reached for the prone knocked-out agent and started patting him down. It didn't take long to find a small case in a pants pocket. I flicked it open and found another adrenaline shot identical to the one Minsheng had used on me and more darts. Not wasting any time, I pulled open the gun's ammo loader and stuffed in the darts.

It had been a while since I'd gone to a shooting range,

but I still remembered enough to get a dart gun loaded. As soon as it was full, I closed the case and stuffed it into one of my pockets, pretty sure another adrenaline shot would be useful given what these agents were firing.

I watched the pair fighting again for a moment, one of them having finally launched an attack. I waited for the right moment and moved a little closer, intending to creep up on the agent or fire as soon as Minsheng had distracted him enough.

As if he'd noticed my intentions, Minsheng danced to his right, moving farther from me. The agent turned. Not hesitating, I fired, getting him in the back with the dart.

He whirled, hissing like a wounded snake. I fired again in panic, and he took another dart to the chest. A moment later, he collapsed.

"Come on," Minsheng said again, waving me toward him.

"Get his dart gun and ammo first," I replied, pulling out the case I'd lifted from the other. With one hand, I tucked it away again, and with the other, I pointed at the matching pocket to the previous agent's stash.

Less than a second later, Minsheng pulled out a similar case.

"Nice," he said, stuffing it into his clothing somewhere I couldn't identify.

With no more agents in sight, we hurried away, both of us jogging at a fair pace.

With all the fighting and the several minutes I'd suffered the effects of the darts, I must have got turned around because we came out at almost the same place I'd gone in. Immediately, the back door of a delivery van opened. Minsheng grabbed my hand and pulled me toward it as someone jumped out.

A short and thin man smiled as he hurried around to the driver's door, glancing our way, the grin getting wider as he got inside.

Minsheng urged me to climb into the back first, the contents of the van putting me off only momentarily. There were rows of tools, including tripwire, traps, and more nets like the one I'd seen earlier. There were even what looked like gas grenades. This man was fitted out for attacking folks.

"Go," Minsheng said as soon as he pulled the van door shut behind us. It grew darker inside, and I had to grab a shelf to steady myself.

I hunkered down as Minsheng's getaway driver stuck his foot on the pedal and got us up to speed and heading off far faster than I'd have liked.

As two more agent cars hurtled past on the other side of the road, ignoring the unremarkable van and heading for the park, I exhaled and sank into a sitting position. I'd gotten away from the agents again. This time with a little bit of help, but once more, Zephyr and I were safe.

CHAPTER FIFTEEN

For a long time, no one spoke. Minsheng panted, sitting down too and leaning against the side wall. The back of the van rattled and bumped, making me feel a little shaken but not stirring Zephyr. I took the time to check on him and make sure he was just sleeping like the last time.

Only once I was satisfied did I look up. Minsheng was looking at the dragon and me.

"We're going to take you somewhere you'll be safe for a while," Minsheng said. "Somewhere I can teach you a few things if you'd like to learn."

I nodded before my brain could catch up. Did I truly trust this man? I didn't know the answer to that question for sure, but I did know he was the first person to help me against the agents trying to catch Zephyr, and he was the first to succeed. Until now, I'd been alone in my fight against them, and the relief of thinking I no longer had to face this on my own almost had tears in my eyes.

If nothing else, a warm bed and a place to rest my feet

were a welcome idea, and so far, so good. But how did I work out if I could trust him for sure?

"Tell me what you meant when you said you thought you'd been waiting for me?" I asked. "You called yourself a *Shishou*."

Minsheng didn't reply at first, instead looking thoughtful and glancing at his companion. The driver glanced back, his eyes a shade of yellow that reminded me of the guy who'd stolen my hairbrush.

I opened my mouth to ask if he was the guy who'd tried to rob me, but I shook my head. It wasn't him, but were they human? I hadn't believed the thought when I'd first had it, but I'd had a dragon hatch out since then and been informed I was an elf with magical abilities.

There was a big part of me that wanted to call someone's bluff or pinch myself and wake up. I had the dragon right in front of me. Accepting he existed wasn't so hard. But elves? I was just me. How could I be an elf?

I was sure of one thing, however. The world had changed around me, and that meant I needed to reassess more than a few assumptions I'd made about how the world worked and where my place was in it.

As I looked back at Minsheng, he finally started talking. "*Shishou* is a Japanese title. It means a master of some kind of skill. I have trained my whole life to aid someone such as you, an elf with gifts so strong that they can bond with a powerful magical creature. In your case, your dragon."

"So, you're like a sensei?" I asked, imagining this guy teaching me martial arts. He'd appeared to know some, although he'd been reluctant to use it.

"Not exactly. 'Sensei' is a word of respect for those in

learned positions—teachers, doctors. It's often used in the western world for someone who teaches martial arts. They don't have to be very skilled at what they do, just in a position of authority in some way."

I nodded, but it was only part of what I wanted to know.

"There is a small organization that has been looking out for your kind and the return of the creatures you bond with for some time. They trained me to aid you, teach you, and help your bond with your creature grow. One day you could be called upon to defend the Earth in a mighty battle. Or you could find yourself in more peaceful times where your mere presence helps to sort out the wrongs of the world as it currently stands."

I snorted in derision. "The former sounds more likely," I replied. "I've been hunted every moment since Zephyr and I bonded. He hadn't even hatched."

"You bonded with him as an egg?" Minsheng asked, his mouth falling open.

"They not teach you the bonding bit?" I asked, thinking he was supposed to be telling me everything as a *Shishou*, not the other way around.

"It's extremely rare for the magic and bond to be strong enough for the creature to bond while still unhatched. Most creatures bond sometime in their first year alive, but it's not something that usually happens right away. How did you make it happen so early?"

"I didn't. I found the egg and kept it. It glowed as I touched it for the first time, leaving my handprint on it," I said, trying to remember what had happened the first time I saw it in the abandoned warehouse.

Minsheng's eyes widened but he didn't respond.

"You also mentioned magic. Like I should be able to do some and do it well." I exhaled as I spoke, still not sure I believed in it, but equally, I was going to see this whole conversation through. Maybe magic could help me.

"I thought you would be able to. To have bonded, you must have the ability. It's not possible without. But you mentioned enough about your past, and your questions now make me believe you were never given a chance to learn." He raised his eyebrows as if he wanted me to confirm, so I nodded. "This is one of the things we will focus on. Can Zephyr fly yet?"

"No, not yet," I replied as the van came to a halt outside a low building among far taller ones. It looked like another restaurant in the Chinatown area of LA.

Minsheng opened the door and offered me a hand to help me out. I took it, grateful, while I still carried the weight of all my belongings and Zephyr on my front. Thankfully Minsheng had made no mention of the small tent I also now carried attached to my bag or the rest of the camping things dangling from the outside. Maybe he'd guessed what my plan had been.

If his words were true and he had been taught all his life to expect me, then, had something guided me to both the dragon and him? And if so, who? Or what? I had so many questions, and I was more than willing to follow Minsheng into the restaurant to get them.

At this time of the day the restaurant was quiet, only a few customers sitting at tables at the far side. Since our getaway driver brought a large box in with him and carried it toward the kitchens with us in tow, we must have looked like nothing more than family friends of the owners or visitors of some kind.

But either way, no one appeared to take notice of us, too absorbed in their own conversations. It helped relax me that the staff bustled around in the kitchen and waved or called a hello to Minsheng and his friend, Chris. I smiled but didn't return anyone's wave. It wasn't meant for me. A few people stared, but most were too polite to show their curiosity so clearly and snuck glances when they thought I wouldn't notice.

Minsheng walked through the kitchens to a small office and then to a staircase beyond that went up and over the restaurant. I followed him up, expecting to find whatever training room he'd mentioned, but instead, all I saw were several bedrooms.

He led me past a couple that were occupied, belongings on dressers or scattered over furniture, then a bathroom and small living room. Lastly were more bedrooms, the final one where we stopped.

After pulling a key from his pocket, he unlocked it.

"This one is yours, should you wish to stay. It's always been here waiting for you," he said, once again confirming he'd been on the lookout for me for a long time.

It was the most luxurious of the rooms I'd seen, the bed low but beautifully made. There wasn't a speck of dust anywhere, and fresh flowers were artfully arranged in a vase on the dresser. A large wardrobe sat on one side of the double bed and a dresser on the other. There was also a large pile of cushions and throws on the floor in the far corner near the window. A desk complete with stationery and all sorts of other useful items, although no computer or laptop, finished off the furniture.

"Let me guess, you had it cleaned and made ready yesterday after you made me dinner?" I asked as I stepped inside.

"No, it has always been ready. We change the flowers every few days. There's always plenty of fresh ones from the restaurant, and the cleaner does all the rooms after she does the restaurant."

"Oh," I said, amazed at the level of effort.

"I'll let you get settled in if you want. I'm in the room at the front of the building. I can wait there until you're ready to see the training facility."

"No," I said. "I can get settled in later. I want to see everything first." I stopped short of saying it was because I didn't fully trust him yet. I didn't want to be rude, especially if he turned out to be the sort of person I'd been looking for my whole life. I'd always sought a teacher—a person who could train me to handle myself.

The sensei who taught me karate had been decent enough, but I'd never fully understood him. Minsheng felt...different. I couldn't put my finger on how or why, but he was far more gentle, unlikely to goad me, although his eyes often twinkled with a mischievous look.

Despite my fears and attempts to be cautious, I was beginning to like Minsheng.

"All right, then," he said as he went past my bedroom. It looked like we were heading to a dead end, only a hatch to the attic there, but he pulled on the ring in the ceiling, and the hatch came down. A ladder descended with it, built in.

Minsheng led the way, flicking a light on as he got up

there. Once I'd followed, finding the hatch hard to navigate with Zephyr strapped to my front, I took a moment to get up beside him.

As soon as we stood in the tiny attic space, I looked around and frowned. There wasn't much room to move up there either. Boxes and other junk lay all over the place, the smell musty and the room far dustier than every other room in the building.

"As Zephyr grows, we'll need to find a new way in, but for now, this will work." Minsheng motioned to the hatch and then turned. I wondered what was up here that could be considered a training ground, but Minsheng made his way around boxes and clutter until he stood at the opposite end of the building.

There was another trap door. I blinked, wondering how hard it was to get to this training facility and where it even was, but he didn't explain, and I was willing to wait and see.

The trap door opened to reveal another steep set of stairs, leading down this time. It was wider than I'd expected and ran down the length of the building. Once more I followed where he led, his hands finding light switches a fraction before I wanted to ask for them.

Down and down we went until I was sure we had gone down far below the restaurant's level. As Minsheng walked through a last door and flicked on the light, he illuminated a room that was almost perfect. It was divided into four sections and must have been underneath the entire building. To my direct left was a dojo, the pillars and floor padded and a row of martial arts-related weapons, guards, and equipment against the far left wall.

To my right was a strange floating assault course with hoops and platforms far up in the air. I could only imagine it was meant for a flying creature.

Farther ahead and to the left was an area I couldn't fathom the purpose of, filled with loads of contraptions with large wooden paddles, and to the far right was a staged area that looked as if it provided a real-life fighting simulation complete with moving sections of walls, dummies, and what might be a robot.

My mouth fell open as I looked around, and Minsheng chuckled.

"You've had all this waiting here for me?" I asked, not sure I could wrap my head around why anyone would do that.

"I have. The organization helped pay for it. I'm one of several *Shishou* around the world waiting for our wards to turn up with their bonded creatures. Here is where you are can train if you want to."

"Want to? I'd love to," I replied, not sure where to begin but desiring to go to all the different areas and try things out.

Minsheng beamed.

"But I still don't understand. Forty-eight hours ago, I was a waitress and a nobody, just making do in one of the craziest cities on Earth. Now you're telling me I'm part elf, can do magic, and this dragon sought me out somehow. I'm also supposed to have met you so you can train me."

"I confess, that kind of thing isn't meant to happen, and has you at a bit of a disadvantage. Normally your parents should have raised you with the knowledge of all this. Of how the world views our kind and what your role in our future might be."

"Well, they didn't. I didn't even know something strange was happening until agents tried to take my egg back in the middle of the night."

"They can be very persistent," Minsheng replied as I dared to put Zephyr down and the bag along with him, although I didn't take my gaze off either. "I'm surprised you've managed to keep away from them as well as you have. Are you sure you haven't had any combat training or anything?"

"I've always been drawn to martial arts," I replied, heading toward the rack of nunchucks and staves.

"That explains a few things," he said as he came up and observed my movements.

"But those agents seemed to want Zephyr and me alive. Are they, like, the FBI or something? Or do they just want to keep the existence of mythical creatures from the awareness of Joe Public?" I asked.

"I wondered when you'd asked why they're attacking you. You're right that they're from an agency, one that tries to keep the creatures secret. Not that there's too many to keep secret. Just the odd people like me and you with DNA that throws anomalies, and my friend. He helped us get away today. Then there's the leftover mythical creatures. Most are small and simple, like mermaids and dryads, fire salamanders, that sort of thing."

"What? Those are all real things?" I asked, feeling like I needed to sit down. Minsheng chuckled as he nodded. I definitely needed to sit down.

Thankfully Zephyr chose that moment to wake and

steal my focus. He rawrled from inside the bag where I'd stuffed him and hurried to get out.

As soon as he realized he was somewhere strange, he got frantic.

"What is it, buddy?" I asked, made wary by his behavior. If he wasn't happy being in the place, it was a possible sign I'd missed something untoward. But Zephyr hurried along the floor toward a door at the opposite end, his nose twitching.

"Oh, have you got him house-trained already?" Minsheng asked, coming with me as I jogged after the dragon.

I didn't reply, not sure what was going on until Zephyr pushed the door open and revealed a toilet. I exhaled, feeling my body relax a little. Zephyr wasn't worried about where we were. He needed to go to the toilet. Again.

Scooping him up, I helped him onto the toilet seat and gave him a moment of privacy. It didn't take him long, and then I was washing my hands. We came back out to see Minsheng setting up some more things in the closest corner. I still didn't dare ask what all the paddles were for, but I had a feeling I was about to find out.

Before I could, Zephyr went sniffing around my bag, and then let out a loud, plaintive roar that made it clear something was wrong.

"He's hungry," I said when he snapped his jaws afterward and continued to sniff the bag, clearly looking for the meat I sometimes carried.

"Of course he is. I'll get the kitchens to send something down to us," Minsheng said as he went over to a small device in the corner. He tapped as if he were ordering on a waiter app and selected a table on one edge of the restaurant selection. "Want anything? Have you managed to get any food since I made you dinner?"

Just thinking of that meal made my mouth water, and I asked for the same again. He grinned and tapped again. I sighed. If I could train down here and keep safe with Zephyr, had a nice cozy bedroom to sleep in each night, and was going to have all my meals cooked for me, I had a feeling I could get used to being here.

For the first time since I'd been fired, I finally felt like things might be okay after all. At least while we worked out how to deal with the agency.

CHAPTER SIXTEEN

Feeling more than a little stuffed, I watched Zephyr waddle around the room investigating. I didn't want to even consider training, but in my defense, if Minsheng had wanted me to be raring to go, he shouldn't have asked the kitchens to send down so much food. It had appeared near the stairs in a dumbwaiter and tasted better than the first time they'd made it for me.

There had been an even bigger bowl of food for Zephyr, tailored to the diet he needed. I guessed the staff was aware there was either a very large dog in their basement or they knew about dragons too. Either way, the thought amused me as Minsheng sent all the empty plates, glasses, and bowls back up to the kitchen.

"Right. I had always imagined you'd come knowing something of every element needed in battle when you arrived, but it's clear you know only one of the four areas well enough to even begin conversing about it."

"Yeah, blame my parents. They dumped me on a

doorstep." I was calmer about these words than I probably ought to have been, but I'd had a long time to get over it.

"Whatever the reason, it means we have to plan where to begin carefully."

"Great. Why don't you tell me what that section's for?" I asked, pointing at the area he'd been tinkering with. He grinned. "And then how about we teach Zephyr to fly? Because a dragon that can't...well, I think he probably needs to."

"Firstly, I'd like to send a sample of your DNA to the organization. I think it would aid our training to know your lineage." Minsheng came a little closer.

I tried not to flinch, wondering what he'd do, but he reached for my hair and plucked several strands. He put them in a small vial and sealed it.

"Oh," I said, understanding making my mouth fall open. "You can do the DNA thing with hair?"

"Only hair that has the follicle attached," Minsheng replied. "And it's best to have at least five."

"Like the kind that falls out naturally and gets tangled in a hairbrush?"

"Yes." Minsheng looked at me, waiting for an explanation of my question and its specifics.

"A short man, thin and almost cat-like, stole my hairbrush a few minutes before I found the dragon egg," I said, gulping. Someone out there knew more about my DNA than I did. Someone out there must have been watching me.

"I'll get this to the organization then," Minsheng said. "And let them know the test is urgent. If there's anything important to know, we want to be the first to know it."

I nodded, not sure what else to say. Fear gnawed at my stomach, making me feel queasy after all the food I'd eaten. I didn't get to dwell on it long, however, since Minsheng came back to me as soon as he'd sent the vial and a note up in the dumbwaiter.

"Don't panic. They can't harm you with the information of your parentage. But knowing will help you prepare and help me know what to teach you and what you will naturally find easiest."

"Then why does someone else want my DNA?" I asked, not buying his reassurances. He frowned and tilted his head, no doubt thinking more carefully this time.

"There are stories of a warrior who will do some very big, very important things at some point in Earth's future."

"Like, a prophecy?" I asked, wanting to laugh at the cliché.

"Sort of. But there's no prophet. It may well just be wishful thinking. And I think we decide our own destinies. Even if you were this person some would fear, you don't have to be. You could choose another path entirely."

"Right," I replied, thinking Minsheng liked to be vague.

"What's most important is that you train and make your bond with your dragon strong; then you will have more paths to choose from. The more you know and master yourself, the more you take control of the world you find yourself in, and the less the winds of change can buffet you from one place to another."

I nodded. That was wisdom and logic I could get behind. I didn't want to run from those agents anymore. I'd had enough of that.

"Let's do this," I said as Minsheng led me over to the paddles. "Let's make me and Zephyr a fighting team."

Although Minsheng briefly grinned, he shook his head.

"Firstly, do you really know nothing of your elven heritage?"

"Until you decided I must be at least part elf, I had no idea they existed outside fairy tales," I replied, wondering where this was going.

"You're part dragon too with those eyes, but we'll get to that another time. The elves are the natural magic wielders of this world. Something about the elements infuses itself in the very DNA of the race. Your element will be air. Or wind. Have you ever found yourself able to move quicker or run faster than another in a fashion you can't repeat?"

I went to shake my head, but when I thought about it, I hesitated. I remembered how others had always declared me fast, yet sometimes my sensei had declared me off my game and riled me to make me angry so that, in his opinion, I'd concentrate and strike faster and more precisely. I realized I had. Slowly, I nodded. And when the agents had given chase over the last few days, I'd been faster. Often.

"Then we at least have a starting point. Let me guess, it was always when you were most emotional?"

Again, I nodded. It was as if he and my old sensei had been talking to each other.

"I want you to concentrate on how it felt the most recent time you think something made you faster and then push your hand toward this paddle without connecting to it. If you tap into the magic within you, it will move."

"Cool," I replied, grinning before I realized I was meant

to be feeling that same focused, determined feeling I had when sensei pushed me.

I pictured the event in my head and heard the sensei's words as he goaded me. Then I thrust out my hand.

"It wobbled," I said, but I knew it was wishful thinking. It hadn't moved. Minsheng didn't bother to speak but pointed at the board as if I should try again. I rolled my eyes.

Once again, I tried to concentrate. This time as I thrust my hand forward and stopped several inches from the wooden paddle, it definitely moved. Zephyr jumped back and forth on his front feet, wiggling his wings and flicking his tail. As far as I could tell, that was his happy dance.

"There we go, Aella-Faye," Minsheng said. "That was magic."

My hand had a slight tingle, warmer now than the rest of me, but I wasn't sure how I'd done it. That Zephyr appeared so pleased made me grin, though.

"Call me Aella," I replied, trying to concentrate and do it again. The third time was only a little wobble again, my concentration clouded.

"Aella, then. You need to think about what you want the air to do as well. That time the air went everywhere. I was wafted with a breeze as if I stood near a lake or on a hilltop."

"Right, so focus and be clear about what the air needs to do," I said softly, as much to myself as to make sure I'd heard him right.

My fourth attempt was a lot more successful. The paddle swung around and smacked my arm hard.

"Ouch," I squealed, but Minsheng laughed.

"It seems you still need to learn control."

I rolled my eyes again, having a feeling I was going to find elements of Minsheng's training annoying. And I was going to have bruises. Lots of bruises.

Over the course of the next half an hour, he had me try more of the same sort of move, moving around the area until I was getting it right most of the time. I still sometimes pushed them too hard or too gently, but every time I tried to do something, the paddles moved at least a little.

Already the feeling of using magic was becoming familiar, something I could imagine and focus on instead of the insults my sensei had hurled at me in the past. I sort of sucked the air toward me and then forced it to go where I wanted it. It was also starting to feel natural, like walking or being able to read.

By the time Minsheng told me to take a break, I was exhausted and more than ready. And hungry. Really hungry, despite it only being an hour or so since we'd eaten.

"So, boss," I said, "how often do I get meals? Can I get snacks?"

"It's Minsheng," he said. "I'm not your employer."

"Can I call you Min? Or Sheng?" I asked, wondering what a suitable nickname might be. He sighed and shook his head. "Sensei?"

"Minsheng or Shishou," he replied, walking over to the tablet where he could order more food. "And you'll be hungrier after doing lots of magic. The energy you'll expend for it has to come from somewhere. The good news is, you'll never be obese. The downside, you'll need to eat the right things."

I sighed at his lack of desire to be called something informal and stroked Zephyr for a bit. The dragon waited while I trained, inspecting the room but otherwise lying on the floor, his tail curled around and under his chin.

"Are there others like me?" I asked. "If there is a whole organization and other Shishou, are there more people like me? Elves and other creatures in hiding?"

"No," he replied. "Not at the moment. There used to be, but you're the first in at least three hundred years. The first I know of, anyway."

I swallowed, taking a moment to think about his words. The only one like me. In the whole world. Could he be right? Or were there maybe others just getting about their lives, waitressing in bars like I was, completely unaware? Was the agency aware of them? Of me? Were they constantly watching for any kind of magic or creature to reveal itself?

"Is that why they want Zephyr so badly?" I asked.

"Perhaps. But whether or not he was unique, they'd be hunting for him. It's their job."

I nodded, feeling lonely. For a moment, I wondered if I'd found a home, but I wasn't quite like Minsheng and the people here. I was still different. I pushed the thoughts aside and tried to think of happier things as the dumb-waiter let out a ping to show more food had arrived.

"So, when do I get to learn how to make fireballs and hurl them at people I don't like?" I asked as he handed me a bowl of soup and a spoon.

I tried to spoon it in too fast and burned my tongue, but he chuckled.

"You don't get to make fireballs. Did you not hear me when I said the elemental magic is fused within your elven DNA? You're clearly descended from someone with strong ties to the air element. You've bonded with a dragon that breathes toxic gas, and you can control the air around you. You'd have had a fire salamander or a phoenix or something if you could make fireballs."

I mock-pouted, not as upset as I wanted to appear. Although a phoenix sounded like an amazing creature to bond with, I was head over heels in love with Zephyr. There was something about the way he looked at me and the cute way he roared. We had also worked together to keep us both safe. He'd paralyzed an agent over my shoulder. Two, actually.

Having a dragon was amazing.

As I looked at him, tucking into his own soup with noisy slurps, I knew that whatever bond existed between us, it was very real and had stolen over me so quickly and completely I didn't think I'd be able to fight it. Not that I wanted to.

"What do the agents do with the creatures they take?" I asked, thinking about how close we'd come to getting caught when Minsheng had turned up.

"I don't know exactly, but I've never seen any again or known of anything that escaped."

I shuddered. They'd almost had Zephyr. They'd almost had me.

"Thank you," I said a moment later, barely able to whisper the words as I kept my gaze fixed on Zephyr. I didn't want to cry, but I could feel my eyes pricking with

AIR BOUND

the threat of tears and a lump forming in my throat. "Thank you for saving us earlier."

"I wouldn't be a very good Shishou if I didn't try to protect you when you needed it most. One day you won't need my help, but until then, I consider myself responsible for your well-being and your skills. If you fail and are taken or killed, I will have failed doubly. Because not only would I have not given my life to save yours, as is my duty, but I would also have failed to prepare you for the challenges you will face."

Minsheng said these words with a set expression on his face, his eyes alight and his mouth forming a firm line with the last word. He meant every part of it.

I nodded, feeling something respond inside me—a stirring in the very depths of my soul that lit up an area long dormant, waiting for this moment. I had a purpose and a destiny, even if I didn't know what they were yet. I also had someone who believed in me. Someone who was dedicated to me.

And I had Zephyr. As he finished, he let out a loud belch and seemed to grin afterward. I laughed as I wrinkled my nose at the smell. Minsheng shook his head, but I noticed the grin that passed across his expression along with the seeming disapproval.

"Come," he said. "Show me you can remember what you've learned, then we will move on."

Sighing as if I thought him a slave driver and disinclined to exert myself again, I got to my feet. Inwardly, I was a mix of emotions. Nerves sent butterflies into my stomach. What if I couldn't do it again suddenly? What if it had been nothing but beginner's luck earlier?

But under my fears was a lot of excitement. This was amazing in its own way. I was becoming more powerful, and the fear I'd had of the agents was dwindling with each new trick I learned.

As I hit the first target again, I proved it wasn't luck and I could remember the feelings that led to me moving air.

"Good," he said, putting his bowl down on a small table. "Now use the air around the bowl to lift it up. Try not to break it."

I blinked, not sure I'd heard him right until he pointed at the bowl and waited. He clasped his hands behind his back and grinned at me.

Taking a couple of long deep breaths, I tried to calm myself. Then I reached out, figuring it would be easier to focus my mind on what I wanted it to do by mimicking it with my hands.

At first nothing happened, but I was trying to be gentle. I didn't want to use too much power and send the bowl flying.

I thought of something more fierce and tried again. This time the bowl wobbled. Growling a little, I imagined something even stronger. This time the bowl lifted, but my control wasn't great. It lurched off to one side a fraction of a second later. Thankfully, Minsheng was on that side and he caught it.

"Again," he said, putting it back. I marveled for a moment at how calm he sounded. Did he care if I broke the bowl, or was it of little importance? Given it was from the restaurant, I could only assume he had hundreds like it.

Thinking that calmed me, and it also made me braver. I tried to lift the bowl again with more haste, and this time it went the other way, falling to the floor and shattering with a loud clatter. Minsheng didn't even look at the many pieces. Instead, he picked up my bowl and put it where the other one had been.

"And again."

My fifth attempt was more controlled, the bowl rising slowly. Minsheng smiled, making me feel delighted, but I lost focus, momentarily more concerned with having his approval than being careful. It dropped on the table and it cracked before breaking in two.

I sighed as he put the broken pieces to one side and placed the third and final bowl there.

"Once more," he said, making it clear I wouldn't be allowed to break any more of the bowls than the few that had been sent down the dumbwaiter with our food.

Doing my best to focus, I took more steadying breaths and locked my gaze on the bowl. A little shakily, I lifted it into the air, moved it around a bit, and then tried to put it back down. I almost missed the table, but I caught it with my mind before Minsheng could and placed it down with only a small clatter.

Exhausted but elated, I grinned at him.

He merely nodded. "Now the first task again."

CHAPTER SEVENTEEN

I smiled as the paddles on the construction in front of me spun in little circles like a weather vane in a stiff breeze.

"You should hook this up to the power lines or something. I could make you some electricity," I said.

Although I'd been joking, Minsheng let out an impressed humph and gave a brief nod, looking as if he was thinking. It wasn't long before he stepped away from that part of the training room.

My gaze followed him as he walked to a different part of the room. He stopped beside a large device made of wood. It looked a bit like a climbing tower for a cat or dog.

I hesitated and Minsheng looked at me, waiting to see if I would follow.

"So, what's this for?" I asked.

"Well, Zephyr needs to fly, doesn't he?" Minsheng replied.

I nodded, grinning. Given how badly our first attempt at flying had gone, I was surprisingly eager to try again. With a trainer on hand, I was sure it would go better.

Zephyr seemed to sense that something was about to happen. Running up to me, he let out a rawrl.

"It's okay, buddy. You can climb this, can't you?" I smiled at him, hoping it would help.

Zephyr looked at the tower as if he wasn't sure what to do. I walked over to it and patted the first platform.

"Come on, just jump up."

Again he looked uncertainly at me. I sighed, then I looked at Minsheng. "Suggestions?"

Minsheng shrugged. I rolled my eyes. Thinking for a moment, I looked at Zephyr and then at the tower. A moment later, I climbed onto the first platform.

"Climb," I said as I got down.

Zephyr opened his mouth in what looked like a smile. A moment later, he climbed onto the platform. Then he looked at me again.

I approached and patted the next one up.

"Climb," I said again.

This time Zephyr got the idea. He put his claws on the front platform and climbed higher. I could only watch as he got higher and higher until he was several feet above me.

"Now tell him to fly," Minsheng said.

"Fly, Zephyr," I repeated, trying to keep the emotion out of my voice and appear like this was normal. I felt more than a little awkward trying to teach a dragon to fly, but I could only assume Minsheng knew what he was doing.

Most importantly, Zephyr was very willing to learn. After wiggling his bottom and moving from one paw to another, Zephyr jumped.

Although he tried to flap his wings, he didn't get any lift and plummeted to the floor. I gasped.

"What are you trying to do?" I demanded, glaring at Minsheng.

"I just taught you to lift something in the air with your magic. I thought you'd help him." Minsheng shrugged.

"You could've told me that was the plan. That could have really hurt him."

"How about we try again? This time you can help."

"With magic?"

"No, with chopsticks. Of course with magic."

I rolled my eyes and helped Zephyr to his feet.

The dragon looked at me, not appearing to be willing to do anything but stare.

"Climb up again," I said, keeping my voice cheery despite my anger. For a moment, he flicked his gaze between Minsheng and me, but eventually, he walked toward the first platform again. Slowly, he climbed back up.

I tried not to panic as he got higher. The last thing I wanted was for him to hurt himself. It had almost broken my heart the first time he'd tried to fly, and that time, he'd landed on soft carpet. This time he was landing on a hard concrete floor.

Taking several deep breaths, I tried to focus on how it felt to perform the needed magic. Maybe I could help him. At the very least I had to try, but I was wary of using too much force. It was clear I could easily overpower his small frame as I had the first bowl.

By the time he reached the top of the tower, my stomach was in knots. I wasn't sure he was doing any better. Once again he moved from paw to paw, flitting back and forth like he wasn't sure what to do. He looked at me, waiting.

I opened my mouth, but nothing came out. How could I ask him to make another jump? Again, I took a deep breath, then I opened my mouth once more.

"Fly," I said.

At first, Zephyr didn't do anything. Then he steadied himself, wriggled his backside, and jumped.

Tapping into the magic I'd felt before, I tried to lift his wings for him. Nothing seemed to help. Once again, he plummeted to the floor. This time he didn't hit as roughly, managing to land on his feet and smile as he did.

I grinned back, feeling like I wasn't an awful dragon parent. At least I'd helped him not hurt himself. Standing a little way from us, Minsheng had his arms folded across his broad chest.

"And again," he said.

Feeling a little better, I nodded. This time I didn't have to ask Zephyr to climb. The less painful landing had given him confidence.

It didn't take Zephyr long to go up. He reached the top and looked at me once more. Taking another deep breath, I lifted my hands and imagined helping him fly.

"Go on, Zephyr," I said. "I've got you this time."

Far less hesitant, Zephyr jumped. I imagined the floating bowl from before and pictured a breeze blowing upward against his wings. This time instead of falling, Zephyr's wings unfolded and he glided several feet across the floor before he landed.

"Yes!" I jumped up and down in delight.

Zephyr turned and looked at me, his mouth hanging open, his tongue to one side. It was clear he was exhilarated. I couldn't imagine what it must have felt like to fly.

Before I could stop him or ask him to do anything else, Zephyr walked toward the tower and began climbing again.

Now eager, he sprang up the platforms. Once again, I took up my position and concentrated. I just hoped I could help him enough.

"Try to make a little less wind this time," Minsheng said.

I nodded. It made sense not to help Zephyr as much. After all, we wanted him to learn to fly, not for me to fly for him. Using magic was taxing, and I wasn't sure how much more I could do that day. With all the training we had done already, my limbs felt heavy, and until Minsheng had mentioned it, I hadn't realized just how tired out I was.

This time when Zephyr reached the top of the tower, he looked straight at me, wriggled his bum, and jumped. It was only a few moments' warning for me to help him. The magic came late, Zephyr falling a little bit before I caught him. The wind buffeted his wings, rocking him off-course, but he soon recovered, flapping and directing himself. I grinned as he managed to land in a skid. It hadn't been graceful, but it had been wonderful. I was helping Zephyr learn to fly.

"Now we're getting somewhere," Minsheng said, a grin on his face as well.

"What do you mean, 'now we're getting somewhere?'" I replied. "He flew last time too."

"The last time, you did it all," Minsheng replied.

I stuck my tongue out. It was a little childish, and I

knew he was right, but I didn't have to appear to agree with him.

Before I knew what was happening, Zephyr was halfway to the top of the tower again. I took another deep breath and tried to focus, ready to help him in a more controlled way. I wasn't going to let him down.

After Zephyr had jumped more times than I could count, I was exhausted. The last few attempts, he had almost flown on his own, but all the magic I'd used had taken its toll. Sitting down, I sighed. I was done.

"That's enough for one day," Minsheng said. "I think everyone is too tired for more."

"You think?" I rolled my eyes. Pushing up from the ground, I got up.

Zephyr didn't move. He panted, and his wings hung limp at his sides. It was clear I wasn't the only one who was too tired to carry on.

"How about some dinner?" Minsheng asked.

"Dinner sounds amazing," I replied.

The thought of more food seemed to help Zephyr too. He stood, tucking his wings away and looking at me.

"Yes, don't worry, you're going to get some food too."

Going to my bag, I realized how much I hurt. Every muscle in my body ached. It was like I'd been to the gym and done a full training routine, one I had never done before. Every inch of me was going to complain about it. If this was how it felt to use magic, I didn't want to do it this much.

"A hot bath and some time to rest," Minsheng said. "That'll make you feel as good as new."

"You'd better hope you're right because if you're not, I'm not sure I'm going to be able to train tomorrow."

"You have to," Minsheng said. "The agents aren't going to rest, so you can't either."

I groaned and grabbed a drink from my bag. Chugging what was left of the water, I already felt a little bit better. Maybe Minsheng was right. I hoped so. I didn't want to feel this exhausted forever. Maybe using magic was like using muscles. The more you did it, the easier it got.

As I put my empty bottle back, Zephyr came up and looked at the bag.

"Do you want to get back in?" I asked.

Zephyr nodded as if he understood my question. I lifted an eyebrow as he pulled himself up the side of the bag. Within seconds he was nestled back where he used to be, curled up on top of my stuff.

"I guess I'm carrying you back up those stairs," I said.

Minsheng laughed and headed that way. I followed, not wanting to be left behind. Although the training room was amazing, it wasn't a place I wanted to be without company. I was also eager for dinner. More than once in the last half hour, my stomach had rumbled. I didn't doubt Zephyr was also as hungry.

As we headed back down the attic steps to the second floor and found ourselves among the bedrooms again, I heard voices. Somewhere in one of the other rooms was a couple talking.

"Why don't you freshen up a moment?" Minsheng suggested. "I'll see about getting you a proper table for dinner."

"Sounds amazing," I said, already heading to my room.

With Zephyr in the bag, there was nothing he could do but come with me, but he looked longingly after Minsheng as the man walked away.

"Don't worry, Zephyr," I added. "We'll go get dinner in a moment."

Again the dragon seemed to understand my words. He hunkered back down in the bag and let me sit on the bed for a moment. I looked at myself in the mirror. Although I'd looked better, I didn't look dead. My hair was ruffled, my limbs hung by my sides, and my clothes sported sweaty patches. It looked like I'd had a workout.

Using the small en suite bathroom, I tidied myself up. As I brushed my hair and tied it up again, I wondered how long the DNA test would take. I was eager to hear more about who I was and who I might be descended from. After all this time, I might even have an answer as to who my parents were.

As the thought popped into my head, a tingle rippled up my spine. More than once in the past, I'd tried to find out who my parents were, but I'd never managed it. No DNA database, ancestry registry, or adoption registry had been able to tell me who my parents were. Of course, I'd told myself it didn't matter. They hadn't wanted me.

But was that true?

Minsheng had said that my kind were hunted. The agency and all the people chasing me confirmed that. Had my parents left me to protect me? Had the dragon egg been hidden in an abandoned building to protect him? I had so many questions and so few answers. But I was going to ask Minsheng every one of them.

By the time I went back downstairs, there was already a

table laid out as Minsheng had suggested. It was in a private room, off to one side of the restaurant, and out of the way. A single table sat in the middle of the room, big enough to sit eight, but it was laid up for seven. As I sat, I wondered who the other five would be.

I didn't have to wonder for long. Minsheng appeared, and with him were several of the staff, including our getaway driver. Zephyr climbed out of his bag and sat on the floor. As soon as they saw him, they stopped.

Everyone watched him for a moment. Clearly, none of them had seen a dragon before. I looked at Minsheng for an explanation. Given how many people had been chasing me to get to Zephyr, I wasn't pleased that so many people were now being made aware of him.

"Hi," I said. My tone was icy. Without knowing who these people were, I was going to be on my guard.

"It's okay, Aella," Minsheng said. "This is my family, and friends who are just like us."

"What do you mean, 'just like us?'"

"People who aren't only human." Minsheng motioned to the driver who had helped us earlier. "This is Chris. He's part gnome. The rest are related to me, and part dwarf or gnome, especially Daisy, my sister." The woman closest to Minsheng beamed at me, her smile lighting her face the same way it did Minsheng's. That was where the family resemblance ended, however. While Minsheng was heavyset and tall, she was thin, almost elf-like, but taller than me.

I was introduced to his whole family, and all of them were warm with their greetings and words. Despite that, I was on my guard. I wasn't used to trusting people, and although these were family, I didn't have much trust in family either. Their presence also made me feel like I couldn't ask questions, not when I didn't know them very well.

Even with my reservations, dinner was wonderful. Unlike the previous occasions, I didn't get to order from a menu, but all the food that had been prepared was put in the middle of the table.

Only then did I realize that the center spun in a circle. Everyone helped themselves to whichever dish they wanted, turning the table or helping others get what they needed by turning it for them. Minsheng sat on my right, explaining what something was if it was a dish I didn't recognize and encouraging me to try them all until he was satisfied I was taking care of myself.

Zephyr also didn't go hungry. Either because feeding a dragon was novel or our hosts were being as kind to him as they were to me, everyone made sure he had plenty of food as well. Whenever his bowl was empty, someone picked up another dish suitable for his palate and offered him a large scoop.

By the time the meal ended I felt more relaxed, less in pain, and full. I sat back, sighing. It was only then I realized that everyone was looking at me.

"What?" I asked.

"We're glad you're here," Minsheng explained. "We've all been waiting for someone like you."

"That's the second time you said you were waiting for me. I don't understand. I don't feel special. I'm just me. Why were you waiting for me?"

"Hope," Minsheng replied. "Hope that things would get better."

I frowned. I wasn't sure I could give anyone hope. Minsheng seemed certain I could, though. Clearly I didn't understand an element he did, but I wasn't about to argue with him in front of his family.

As dessert was brought out, everyone moved on. I hadn't thought I could eat any more, but the smell of hot apple pie soon had me tempted.

The conversation returned to normal topics, talk of food prices, politics, and running a restaurant until, eventually, we were all done.

Two of the older women collected the plates and discussed who would do the washing up. I raised an eyebrow, surprised they didn't have a dishwasher, but I wasn't about to volunteer. I had questions, and Minsheng was going to answer them.

I was pretty sure Minsheng realized we had more to talk about. When the others got up, most of them leaving, he stayed beside me. I sat back, picked up my glass so I would have something to focus on, and looked at him.

"Thank you for agreeing to stay this time," he said. "I know that can't have been easy for you."

"It's not like I've got anywhere else to go," I replied, shrugging. Now that it came to it, I wasn't sure how to ask all the questions I had or if they were questions he could answer. My world had been turned upside down. I didn't even know who I was anymore.

"You should get some rest. We'll need to train more tomorrow."

"I know," I said, staring at the last gulp of water in my glass, feeling it warm between my fingers. "I will. I don't want to be running from these agents forever. But I don't want any harm to come to Zephyr. While he's so small and vulnerable, I need to keep him safe. And I don't intend to trust people I don't know very well. Already, even those I'd hoped would be safe to be with unknowingly put us in danger."

"Your bond to Zephyr is strong for such a short time. That's a good sign. And I mean it when I say that you're safe here. No one would betray you." Minsheng's voice was gentle, but I could hear the certainty in it. He believed his words to be true.

Nodding, I put the glass down and got up.

"Let me know the second you get my DNA results back," I asked as I walked toward the door.

"Of course. Rest well, Aella."

"Rest well, Shishou."

CHAPTER EIGHTEEN

The sun's rays streaming in through the window woke me the following day. I blinked and yawned before looking for Zephyr. He was curled up on the bed as well, snoring softly, his head resting on his tail.

For a moment, I watched him. Sometime in the night, he'd climbed onto the bed with me, nuzzling against me and resting there. I hadn't objected, feeling the warmth of his body and enjoying the soft snores, the sound almost like a cat's purr.

When I'd come up to the room the night before, I'd found a bath already run, full of bubbles and alluringly scented. Luxurious baths weren't normally my thing, but something about sinking into it had eased the aches and pains, and I'd slipped between the cool bed sheets with gratitude for whoever had prepared both for me.

I'd been watching Zephyr for some minutes, thinking about the last few days, and trying to remember what I wanted to ask Minsheng and make sure I learned from him when there was a knock on the door.

"Give me five," I said, pushing back the covers and getting up. With very little clothing to change into, I did the best I could and made a mental note to try to find a place to get more clothes. I had some money now, at least. With all that done, I tucked my items back into my bag, hiding half the money in there. I'd hidden the other half around the room in various places.

Minsheng appeared honorable, and he'd rescued me and was teaching me how to defend myself. But he hadn't given me the key to my room yet, so I wasn't leaving anything valuable on show, especially when I didn't have a lot.

As soon as I was halfway decent, I rushed to the door, unlocked it, and pulled it open. Minsheng stood there, holding a tray of breakfast for the dragon and me.

I grinned and backed up as he came in and set it on the dresser.

"Find a perch and tuck into this. I've got your DNA results, and you're going to want to be sitting down." Minsheng handed me the smaller of the two bowls of oatmeal and a spoon, leaving the toast, marmalade, and fruit on the tray. I wasn't going to argue with the order of consumption but sat back down on the end of the bed, cross-legged.

Zephyr finally woke up, sniffing the air as he let out an appreciative rawrl.

His tail thumped the bed a few times as Minsheng placed the larger bowl of oatmeal on the floor. Within seconds, Zephyr had half-jumped and half-flown down to the floor to eat.

Blowing on the first spoonful, I moved my gaze to my

mentor. He pulled a piece of paper out of his pocket and scanned it, reaching the bit he was looking for.

"As we suspected, you're a mix of elven and dragon, but you're also part human. The interesting element of note is your line of ancestry," Minsheng said before pausing.

"Go on," I replied, hoping he'd hurry up and get to what he seemed to think was the good part.

"You're descended from Tuviel the Great and the line of dragons she bonded with."

"So, they somehow had babies together?" I replied, my mind going to interesting places.

For a moment, Minsheng was so lost in laughter that he couldn't talk, let alone answer my question. I tried to wait for him to calm down without showing my impatience, feeling like the joke had been at my expense. When I folded my arms across my chest, my bowl resting on my legs, Minsheng finally pulled himself together.

"Sorry," he said. "I forget you know so little of what I speak about. Dragons, when fully grown and accessing their entire genetic memory, can take human form. As such, there is no difficulty with them pairing with someone from the other major races. While as far as I'm aware, Tuviel didn't have children with the dragon she bonded with. One of her descendants clearly paired with a descendant of her dragon."

"Right," I replied, feeling my cheeks grow hotter as we discussed who had been fooling around with whom to make me. "But why is that so important? Who is Tuviel?"

Minsheng sighed. "I think there needs to be some reading on our regular activities list. Tuviel is one of the greatest air-elemental elves ever to have existed. And her bond with her dragon Azargad was phenomenal. They could communicate in a way that made them an effortless team. They flew together regularly. She protected this world from extinction more than once."

I swallowed. Those were some big boots to fill for someone normal like me.

"But that's not all. You have human DNA, which comes from so varied and large a population and runs in you in too small a quantity to match to any one person. So that's not very interesting. But you have dragon and elven DNA from another source as well. Perhaps several other sources."

"So what you're saying is, I'm a mongrel of three different races and a whole heap of important ancestors."

"No. Oh, Aella, quite the opposite. You have the blood of at least four different powerful beings running through you. You're anything but a mongrel. If we're keeping to the analogy, you have a fantastic pedigree."

I blinked, not sure I understood.

"You have the potential for greatness within you, Aella-Faye. If I hoped before that you could grow into a protector for the Earth, I'm sure of it now. I'd like to run Zephyr's DNA through the organization's database as well."

I shook my head immediately, shifting closer to the dragon still wolfing down his breakfast. He had moved on to the large chunks of grilled ham and vegetables Minsheng had brought up for him.

"If we're trying to hide for a while, I don't want any more people knowing I have a dragon. It's bad enough that your family knows. If I had my way, no one would know."

"Is your decision out of fear or wisdom?" Minsheng asked, studying me. I looked away, feeling like his gaze looked directly into my soul. It was fear. I didn't want anyone else coming after Zephyr. At least, not until I'd dealt with the threat I already had. But just because it was fear, it didn't mean it wasn't also wisdom.

"The organization already knows you have a dragon," Minsheng said after a moment, as if he was trying to reassure me.

I frowned. I didn't want to admit that Minsheng was right.

"All right," I replied. "What do you need?"

"The best thing is a scale," Minsheng said. "But we can wait until he sheds naturally."

I nodded, ready to get on with the day. I wanted to train more, and I really needed to get some clothes. When I told Minsheng about the latter, he raised his eyebrows.

"Are you sure? I could—" he started to reply.

"I am not letting anyone buy my underwear for me," I said as I folded my arms across my chest.

"The agents are still looking for you. I don't recommend you go out."

"They have no idea I'm here, so it's not going to be easy for them to find me. Besides, I'm just going to go get some underwear and a few T-shirts, maybe a pair of pants. It is not like I'm gonna be more than a few minutes."

Minsheng's mouth became a thin line, but he didn't protest this time. As I grabbed my bag and encouraged Zephyr into it, he lifted his hands.

"I think it's best to leave Zephyr," Minsheng said. "You'll be quicker, and it is better if you're not both in danger."

"The two of us go everywhere together," I replied. "And that's not up for debate. Zephyr bonded with me, and I won't leave him somewhere I can't see him."

Minsheng sighed and shook his head. "It seems there's no arguing with you. I just hope you know what you're doing."

"I just want clothes," I said. "And I won't be long. Then we can train as much as you want. We have an agency to beat."

He nodded, a small smile appearing on his face.

As soon as Zephyr was in the bag and curled up, I lifted it onto my shoulders. The dragon was definitely growing. The extra weight on my shoulders made them ache, and I knew I wouldn't be able to do this much longer.

Minsheng went with me to the front door, grabbing the keys to a car on the way.

"I'll give you a lift to some clothes shops," he said. "Then I'll drive around the block and pick you up when you're done."

I grinned. It made me a lot less nervous to know he would be waiting for me. Despite my bravado, I felt more than a little nervous about going out into the world again and facing the agents. I only got away from them last time because Minsheng had been there to help me. I might be able to do magic now, but I was a long way from being able to use it in battle.

It didn't take long for Minsheng to get me to a clothes shop. I rushed inside, going straight to the sections I needed. Within seconds, I was picking out whatever would do. Zephyr peered at what I was carrying, still on my front.

Thankfully the shop was quiet, and no one seemed to notice I had a dragon in a bag in front of me.

I didn't bother trying anything on but paid for it all without hesitation. It used up some of the precious money I had left, but I needed clothes. I also didn't think I could go back to my apartment yet. It was one of the few places the agents knew I might go.

When I left the shop, I looked for Minsheng in his car. At first I couldn't see him, and a knot formed in my stomach. I didn't want to be out in the open more than I needed to be. I also realized I had no way of contacting Minsheng. Even though I had a phone, I couldn't use it. And he hadn't given me his number anyway. In fact, I'd never seen him use a phone either. Did he have some other way of contacting people?

When I saw a dark car coming up the road toward me, I almost turned and fled straight back into the shop. Was that an agent? Had I been found again? But it drove past, and nothing else happened. Exhaling, I felt the tension leave my shoulders again—just a false alarm.

No sooner had I thought that than Minsheng's car pulled up to the curb in front of me. I'd never been more grateful than I was at that moment.

"Got everything you need?" he asked.

"Yep," I replied, grinning.

As I went to put my shopping bag on the back seat, I noticed there were other bags there already. Groceries from a market or something. I guessed I wasn't the only one who had been shopping.

It didn't take us long to get back, and I was eager to get started. We dropped off the stuff, taking his groceries to the kitchen and my clothes to my room, and headed to the training room.

As soon as Zephyr realized where he was, he let out a delighted little rawrl. He scurried around the room, sniffing everything and wiggling his tail.

"Let's see how much you remember from yesterday," Minsheng said as he walked over to the wooden paddles.

I grinned as I nodded. This I could do. There was something about using my magic that made me feel alive—like I was designed to do it. As I focused, warmth spread through my body.

Within seconds I had the paddles moving, most of the air in the room under my control.

"Well, you clearly remember how to do that." Minsheng moved back to the area of the room meant for Zephyr. "Why don't we see how well our little dragon remembers to fly?"

Zephyr roared and ran to the tower. He climbed it in no time. Once again, I concentrated on my magic, but Zephyr jumped before I had a chance to activate it.

With his wings outstretched, Zephyr flew. My mouth fell open as he glided about the room. Here was my little dragon, flying. I felt exhilarated just watching him.

"Seems you've both benefited from a good night's sleep and some decent food. I did hope you might."

"Not worrying where you're going to get your next meal from and if you might get caught every five seconds does wonders for the ability to recover," I replied, knowing I sounded snarky. It wasn't his fault, but I felt a small amount of resentment that I hadn't been able to protect us or find us somewhere safe.

"Let's learn a few new things, then," Minsheng said, thankfully ignoring my response and defusing the situation.

As he moved toward the part of the room that was set up for fighting, the dojo area, I smiled. Minsheng was a taskmaster, but I was glad to have someone teaching me. Especially someone who appeared to know what I needed to calm down.

"Now, I know you know how to fight. I've seen you in action. But let's see if you can combine the two, magic and martial arts."

I moved closer as Minsheng attached several padded pieces of equipment to himself. It was clear he was expecting to get hurt.

While Zephyr continued to fly round the room, I prepared to spar with Minsheng. Unlike my previous sensei, he didn't bow but beckoned me closer.

"Attack me," he said. "But use your magic and your usual fighting techniques. Try to overwhelm me with both."

"You sure?" I asked.

He nodded, but I could see a hint of worry in his eyes.

I paused for a moment, thinking. Using my magic would make it easy, but I couldn't use my magic all the time. Already I felt tired, and I'd only been using it for a few hours. But battles were often short, and that meant I could use it sparingly.

Concentrating, I imagined the air knocking him off his feet. Either summoning enough wind for a person required more energy, or I wasn't ready to hurt him because he only wobbled, the wind ruffling his hair and making his clothes billow out behind him.

He chuckled and came closer. I lifted my arms to defend myself just in time. He lunged, and I blocked. For the next few minutes, we sparred, neither of us getting a shot in, neither of us letting our guard down.

"Add in the magic," he said, growling the last word.

I considered a clever retort, but given how badly my last attempt had gone, I thought better of it.

Instead, I focused on how it felt to use the magic again. I needed to get enough wind up that I could knock him off his feet. Heat rushed to my hands until they felt like furnaces. With everything I had, I pushed it forward.

He flew backward, landing with a bump. My hands went up to cover my open mouth. I'd sent him flying, and not in a good way.

"I am sorry," I said. "Are you all right?"

He chuckled as he pushed to his feet, the padding making it harder to get up.

"That is what I meant," he said, smiling despite how much that must have hurt.

I almost offered to spar again, but that one attempt to knock him off his feet had drained me. I wasn't sure I could do it again. At least, not yet.

"Why don't we take a break?" he suggested.

"And have a snack?" I asked.

"And have a snack," he said, grinning as he shook his head.

As I sat down at the edge of the room, Zephyr came to join me. He rested his head on my lap and flopped down beside me. I guess I wasn't the only one tired out by the morning's activity.

"So, how are we doing?" I asked as Minsheng handed me a bowl of popcorn.

"As well as I'd hoped," Minsheng replied. "You have the blood of very powerful elves running through you; I'd have expected no less than for you to master your element. The hard part will be learning to control it and have the energy to do it as often as you're going to need to."

"You think I'm going to need to do it that much?"

"I fear so. I hope not," he said, giving me a wan smile.

CHAPTER NINETEEN

"Tell me about Tuviel and Azargad," I said when we finished eating. "What were they like? When did they live? I want to know more about them."

"I've got a book on them if you'd like to read it," Minsheng said. "But they were the greatest bonded pair ever known on Earth."

"But there is no mention of them in any of the mythologies, at least not the ones I've read. How can they have been so great when no one knows about them?"

"Present-day governments don't want us to know that mythological creatures still exist. They were erased from our history, and just to cover their backs in case something slipped through their censoring, they left the really old stuff in, banking on the fact that too much time has passed for anyone to be able to make the link between legend and reality. I'm not surprised you've never heard of Tuviel and Azargad, but their stories are told among those who know. Those of us with dwarven and elven heritage still talk about them. Most of the stories are passed down orally, but there are a few books if you know where to get them."

I nodded, not sure what to think. Part of me still couldn't quite believe that beneath the façade of a normal human existence, mythological creatures mixed, bonded, and thrived, and no one knew about it. Or was it just that I hadn't met anyone who knew? Sighing, I got back up.

"If I'm to be like them, then I'd best keep training."

Before Minsheng could rise, there was a strange beeping from a box on the wall.

"What's that?" I asked. Minsheng rushed to his feet, the open-mouthed and wide-eyed look on his face confirming what I already suspected. It was something bad. Something very bad. And there was only one bad thing that could happen to me here.

The agents. They'd found us.

Guilt hit me like a tidal wave. There was just one way they could have found us. My little shopping trip must have led them right to us. I was to blame.

"Agents?" I looked at Minsheng, hoping he wouldn't confirm my thoughts.

"Agents," he replied. Grabbing my arm, he tried to pull me toward the far end of the training room. "We need to get out of here. We need to get you somewhere safe."

"What about the others?"

"They'll delay them as long as they can," Minsheng replied. "But we must hurry."

Again, I resisted. There was no way I was running away when I had caused this. I was tired of running away, and I wasn't doing it today.

"No," I said. "We're going to help your family."

Minsheng looked at me, clearly thinking about objecting, but he didn't protest.

"All right," he said eventually. "If you think you're ready."

"I have to stand up to them at some point."

"I'll help you as much as I can."

"Zephyr, come on," I said, motioning for the dragon to come with me. "It's time to make them regret coming here."

Not waiting for Minsheng to follow, I climbed back up to the top of the attic. Once we were there, we could hear the fighting, screams, and people running outside.

Minsheng insisted on taking the lead. Feeling a little less confident, I let him. We hurried down to the second floor and to the small flight of stairs that lead to the kitchen.

"Where are they?" a male voice asked.

"I told you, I don't know who you mean," one of the waitresses replied.

There was the sound of a hand striking flesh and a soft gasp.

"I won't ask again. Where are they?"

I rushed downstairs, not waiting any longer.

"Here," I replied before anything else could happen.

An agent stood in the kitchen, holding onto Daisy's hair and bending her neck back. A red mark bloomed on her cheek where he'd struck her.

"Let her go," I said, moving farther into the room. I concentrated on gathering the power I needed, my hands beginning to tingle, heat growing. Beside me, Zephyr growled.

I didn't know how many other agents there were, but as

he let Daisy go and reached for a holster on his side, I released the energy. A blast of wind knocked him off his feet and he flew back, clattering into the counter. Pots and pans fell on his head, each one making him grunt.

Minsheng rushed to help his sister to her feet.

"How many more are there?" he asked.

"At least seven more," she replied, her voice calm despite the danger she'd been in only moments before. "I thought you were going to run away."

"I'm not going to let them hurt you," I said. "I'm not going to be hunted anymore."

Before we could try to find the rest, the agent got up, shedding pots and pans as he rose to his feet. He wobbled, still disoriented. Daisy didn't give him a chance to get his wits together. Grabbing the nearest frying pan, she smacked him on the head with it. He went down like a sack of potatoes.

I grinned, glad I wasn't the only one who was willing to fight back. As the clatter of furniture being thrown and the sound of wood breaking came from the room next door, I looked at Minsheng. We needed to go help.

As one, the three of us rushed into the main dining room. The few remaining customers were hiding under tables at one edge of the room, and the agents were locked in battle with the staff.

Zephyr launched at the nearest agent, exhaling a cloud of gas. The agent froze partway through throwing a punch. The chef in front of him shoved the paralyzed body over.

Before I could decide on a target of my own, an agent leaped at me. Blindsided, I almost went down. Putting a hand out behind me, I imagined air propping me up. A gust of wind blew into me from behind, pushing me back into the agent.

He lifted his eyebrows in surprise, hesitating. I seized the advantage and gave him a roundhouse kick to the side. He doubled over.

Close by, Daisy wielded her frying pan again, finishing the agent off. This time I grabbed his gun, no doubt loaded with darts, and handed it to her.

"It should be full of tranquilizers," I said when she stared at it. She took it, nodding.

As another agent wrestled with the chef who had helped me earlier, I reacted. Using the force I could muster for only a few moments, I sent a blast of wind at the agent.

It was so fierce he flew off his feet, smashed into the table behind, and broke it. He didn't get up again.

Minsheng overpowered another agent, and that left just four that I could see. I rushed over to the nearest one.

The agent stood in the middle of the room, his gun in his outstretched hand. While he was trying to aim at another one of the staff, I hurried up behind him.

I caught my leg on some debris, tripping and stumbling without falling over. The noise drew my target's attention and he whirled, bringing the gun to bear on me.

Before he could fire, I punched upward, trying to use the air to add speed and power to my move. Just quickly enough, I caught the gun and sent it flying out of his grasp.

He shook his hand as if his fingers stung, but the reprieve was temporary. I didn't get another hit in before he was on the defensive.

For about half a minute, we dodged around, neither of us managing to hit the other. As I had when sparring with

Minsheng, I tried to use magic and blast him with air. Either I'd exhausted my power, however, or I just couldn't concentrate enough because nothing happened.

A strange noise from Zephyr drew my attention. I looked his way to see him struggling with another agent. I turned to run to his aid, but the agent I was fighting grabbed my arm and spun me around.

Anger and fear filled me, making my hands grow hot. Instinctively, I knocked him over with a large blast of air.

Free once more, I ran to Zephyr.

The dragon had his jaw locked on the leg of the agent, but the man was doing everything he could to make Zephyr let go. Grabbing at the dragon as he tried to wriggle, he caught hold of the tip of one wing.

Zephyr let go, trying to get away. As the agent lifted him, I barreled into the man, and all three of us went over. Using my powers in the same way I had earlier, I pushed up from the floor. Before the agent could get up, I shoved my hand up against his neck, turning his face toward Zephyr.

"Breathe on him, Zephyr," I said.

Thankfully, the dragon thought the same. By the time I finished speaking, out came a cloud of gas. The agent inhaled before he knew what was happening.

I went to Zephyr and checked that he was okay. He let out a rawrl and unfurled his wings to show me no damage had been done.

Ready for the next target, I looked around the room. The agents appeared to be overwhelmed and outmatched. They took one look at me, the dragon at my side, and the scene around them and ran.

Minsheng, Zephyr, and I hurried after them. I reached the threshold of the restaurant in time to see the last few agents grab their fallen comrades and hurry into the cars. Feeling so tired my limbs ached, I just watched them go.

"That wasn't much of a fight," I replied. Then I looked around.

The restaurant had been decimated. Everywhere there were broken tables, broken glass, or distraught customers. It was going to take an age to clear it up.

Minsheng helped another person to their feet as everyone stared at me. I gulped.

Suddenly, I wished the floor would swallow me. This family had taken me in, fed me, and treated me like a very welcome guest. My actions had probably cost them their livelihood.

"I'm sorry," I said. "I am so sorry."

"This isn't your fault. You didn't ask them to hunt you." Minsheng picked up a chair that had somehow survived and set it on its feet.

"No, I didn't ask them to come after me, but you told me not to go to the shop this morning, and I didn't listen," I replied. "This is all my fault."

Zephyr seemed to sense my distress. He came up beside me and rested his head against my leg. I reached down and picked him up, hugging him.

As I looked around, I realized there were still customers in the restaurant. All of them stared at Zephyr as if they'd seen a ghost, and for many of them, I didn't doubt this was the first time they'd seen a dragon. But I wasn't the only one who noticed the customers' interest and fear. Now that the danger was gone, the rest of the staff encouraged the customers out from underneath the tables, assuring them that everything was okay.

Some of them didn't look convinced, their gazes still fixed on Zephyr. I froze, not sure what to do.

"Come," Minsheng said, motioning for me to go back upstairs with him.

"Do we need to go somewhere else now? To be safe?" I asked as soon as we were alone in my room.

"Possibly," Minsheng replied. "But we'll come back to that."

"I'm sorry they wrecked your restaurant," I added, unable to get over it. "I don't have any money to pay for it."

Minsheng chuckled. "It's okay, Aella. The organization will pay for it. They have insurance for this kind of thing."

I felt a little better. I didn't know what the organization was, but Minsheng seemed to think they'd help. It would still take a while to fix the restaurant, though, and I said as much.

"Yes, it will take a little while, but this is where tourists congregate. In a few weeks, no one will even remember what happened."

"They've all seen Zephyr," I said, unconvinced.

"No doubt my family is now telling them it was a large dog or some other kind of pet," Minsheng replied.

I sat down on the edge of my bed, not sure how I felt about the fight. Everything had happened so fast, and so much had been destroyed.

Zephyr got up on the bed beside me, curled up, and put his head on my lap once more. Absentmindedly, I stroked him, the feel of his bronze scales soothing.

"I want to stop this from happening," I said eventually. "I've had enough."

"What do you mean?" Minsheng asked.

"I want to get them to leave me alone. I want to show them they're not getting Zephyr back."

"You want to attack them?"

"Yes." I got up, fear and excitement turning my stomach into a twisted mess. "I want to take the fight to them."

"Are you sure you're ready?"

I shook my head. No, I wasn't sure I was ready, but I wasn't as tired as I thought I'd be after using all that magic. The training was already having an effect.

"There's a lot to organize," Minsheng said, sitting down on the only chair in the room.

"I know. We don't even know where their headquarters are, or who they report to."

"Or how many of them there are," Minsheng pointed out.

"So let's find out," I replied.

Minsheng studied me for a moment while I sat there and waited. I was determined not to run anymore, and I didn't want others to get hurt because of me either. Anywhere we ran to, I was sure they would follow. How many places on Earth could I let be destroyed for my protection? This chase would never end unless I made it end *now*. Attacking them was the only sensible option as far as I could see, but I couldn't pull off something like that alone. Not even with a dragon.

"Will you help me?" I asked.

"Of course," Minsheng replied, a strange light in his eyes. "After today, I'd be delighted."

CHAPTER TWENTY

Down in the training room once more, I worked with Minsheng and Zephyr to make sure the dragon and I did the best we could. For now, we were waiting.

Since the restaurant had been destroyed, we'd been discussing a plan of attack, but it all fell down at the first hurdle. We didn't know enough about the agents.

Although I'd swiped one of their radios the first time I'd attacked an agent outside my apartment, I didn't have it anymore. Neither did I think it would work to listen in. The device had been missing for ages. Surely they'd have changed frequency by now, at the very least.

But the attack had delivered us an alternative that might work. One of the agents had been left behind, out for the count.

"Do you think we should interrogate him?" I asked when we took a break from our training.

"He's not likely to tell us anything." Minsheng shrugged.

"I have no desire to torture anyone," I replied, thinking about how to interrogate someone.

"I have heard that doesn't work anyway."

While I tried to think of another solution, I watched Zephyr fly around the room. Already he could lift off the ground without needing to jump off something, and he seemed to delight in being in the air far more than he liked to walk across the floor. My eyes followed him, wondering what it would be like to fly. Saying I was envious would be an understatement.

"What if we let him go?" Minsheng asked.

"Just...let him go?" I replied. I turned to look at Minsheng, wondering what he was thinking.

"And follow him. What if we let him escape and follow him wherever he goes? We could find out where his head-quarters is and how many agents are there. We might even learn if they have other mythical creatures there." Minsheng looked at me. "What do you think?"

I thought about it for a moment, trying to imagine how we could go about it. Eventually, I nodded.

"Okay. But when it's dark." I wanted to say it was a strategic idea, but it was getting late in the day, and I'd been using lots of magic. I wanted dinner first.

"That gives us time to plan and prepare." Minsheng led the way back to the rest of the house. It seemed the training was done for another day.

I called to Zephyr, trying to get him on the floor again. At first he wouldn't land, giving me a cheeky grin as he flew around the room. As I began walking up the steps, he flew over my head and landed at the top.

Shaking my head but smiling, I followed him up. When I got to the top, I picked him up. I groaned under the weight but made my way up the ladder to the attic.

"You're getting heavy," I said, putting him down on the attic floor. "You're on your own now."

"He keeps growing like that, we're gonna have to find another entrance."

"Why isn't it big enough for a dragon?" I asked, having thought that since the beginning.

"All the other mythical creatures an elf could have bonded with are much smaller. Well, most of them are. Apparently, someone bonded with a kraken once."

I opened my mouth but had no idea how to respond. It seemed every few hours I learned about something new. A new creature, a new person, something they had hidden in history. I was beginning to question everything I'd been taught.

By the time we got downstairs and told our plan to everyone we'd need, it was time for dinner. Once more, I sat down at the five-member family. This time the gnome descendant didn't join us.

"Where is your friend?" I asked, leaning toward Minsheng and keeping my voice down.

"He's gone to find us a few supplies. Walkie-talkies, night-vision goggles. That sort of thing."

I nodded as if that was normal information. In reality it was another weird part of my new life. I'd gone from a waitress to someone plotting to track down an agency and taking care of them. Well, at least send a message. I didn't really want to kill anyone.

As soon as we finished eating—the meal even more delicious than the previous day's—Minsheng motioned for me to follow him.

They'd kept the agent in the pantry and the restaurant

was closed for the rest of the day, but it was a temporary solution at best.

"You take this in to him?" Minsheng said, handing me a bowl of soup. "And see if you can get him to talk. Of course, it doesn't matter if he talks or not. We just want him to think we're interrogating him."

I wanted to ask why me. Instead, I took the bowl of soup and walked toward the door.

"Zephyr, stay here." I motioned for the dragon to stay where he'd settled himself on top of one of the kitchen counters. At first I thought he'd disobey me, but he put his head down on his front paws as if he were waiting for me to come.

I nodded at Minsheng to let him know I was ready. He moved the chair holding the door shut, and I reached for the handle.

After taking a deep breath and thinking about what to say, I walked into the room. The agent was strapped to a chair and gagged. Without the sunglasses, I could finally see what he looked like.

This particular agent had deep blue eyes and a large Roman nose. It was clear he was angry about having been captured. For a moment I paused in front of him, holding the bowl of soup.

"I am sure you'll be hungry by now," I said as I took the gag off. "Why don't you tell me why you are hunting me, and I'll let you eat it."

"So, you're starting with bribery?" he asked, his voice deep. It had a slight Texas twang.

"Gotta start somewhere." I leaned against the side wall, acting as if I had plenty of time. "How about I tell you something, then it's your turn. I stumbled upon a giant egg abandoned in a warehouse, so I did what any good citizen would do. I took the egg home, kept it warm, and tried to find out what it was. I was thinking, 'I can give it to the ASPCA' or something like that, and I'd have done my good deed for the day. Next thing I know, there's a bunch of men like you hunting me down. *Then* I meet the guy here, and I'm told that fairies are real and you guys are trying to cover it up."

The agent laughed, almost snorting. I waited for him to stop. There was no way I was going to let him see he was getting to me.

"I've seen magic before," he finally said. "And you've clearly been doing it a lot longer than three days."

I raised an eyebrow. Did I appear to be that good at magic? Or was he just trying to make out that it was my fault?

"You know you can't cover this up, right?" I looked at him as I spoke, studying him. "Loads of people saw the dragon today."

"Seeing something like that from a distance once, briefly? All of them are going to tell themselves they saw something else. And if they don't and start talking about it on social media or in emails, people they know will doubt them just enough so they'll begin to doubt themselves."

"Let me guess. Anyone else that gets more insistent will be branded as crazy by everyone else."

"That's what usually happens."

"It's not what is going to happen now. This time." Stepping forward, I put the bowl of soup down on his lap.

He looked down at the bowl for a moment, his hands

still tied to the chair. And then he looked at me. Unless I helped him, he couldn't eat it.

It was the only way I was comfortable torturing someone, and in truth, I wasn't sure I'd call it torture.

"I want you to leave me alone," I said, deciding to stick with the truth. "I didn't ask for any of this."

"Hand over the dragon, and we'll leave you alone."

"If you know about magic, then you know dragon has bonded to me. I couldn't give you him if I wanted to."

"Then my team is going to keep coming."

I rolled my eyes. Why were people so black and white? For a moment, I considered arguing or asking him something else, but I knew it would be a waste of my time.

"Now, I'm pretty sure you're not the boss. So, are you just following orders? And if so, who is giving them?"

"You really don't have a clue, do you?"

I folded my arms across my chest. This was going nowhere. Sighing, I walked out of the room, leaving the bowl of soup on his lap. Minsheng raised an eyebrow, looking into the room and taking in how I'd left the agent.

"Don't ask," I said after shutting the door. Zephyr jumped off the kitchen counter and came straight to me. "There's only one way we're solving this."

I made a fuss of my dragon, stroking him and praising him, relieved to see him. Since the moment he'd hatched, he'd not been out of my sight for even a minute. And although I'd only been on the other side of the door, I now felt relieved that we were together again.

"Do you want to take the first watch to see when he escapes? Or do you want me to?" Minsheng asked.

"I'll do it," I replied. "It'll keep me from falling asleep.

Apologize to your sister for me, though. There's gonna be a bowl of soup to clear up."

Minsheng chuckled as he walked away, leaving me to hide behind the kitchen counter. Once more I considered sending Zephyr away, but I couldn't bring myself to do it. One parting a day was enough.

"Looks like we've got some waiting to do," I whispered. Almost immediately, Zephyr settled down beside me, leaning his body against my legs. For now, everything felt right again.

It didn't take long before we heard scraping and the occasional little bump. A few minutes later, the soup bowl clattered to the floor.

With a quiet sigh, I got to my feet. Zephyr joined me, and I waited in the darkening kitchen. It still wasn't pitch-black outside, and I wasn't sure the rest of the house had gone to bed yet, but there was no way the agent could have known that. He'd been out cold for a long time and would no doubt be wondering what time of the day it was.

After the clatter of the bowl and the splatter of the soup it had contained, there were no more sounds for several minutes. The agent was far more cautious than I would have been.

I tried not to yawn as I began to feel tired.

Come on, I thought. *Get out here so I can follow you back to base.*

Almost as if the agent had heard me, I saw the door handle slowly turn. I backed up, making sure as little of me could be seen as possible. It would give the game away if he spotted me.

As soon as the agent emerged into the kitchen,

crouching down so he was harder to spot, he looked around. I pulled back, listening to the sounds of his movements.

He didn't make much noise, no doubt trying to be stealthy. A little scrape here and a scuffle there let me know he was on his way to the front of the restaurant.

I hurried after him, keeping crouched as well. I'd only gotten as far as the kitchen door when I heard voices.

"So, you're going to stop me?" the agent said as he stood up, straightening his back and lifting his chin.

I couldn't see who he was talking to. The agent was looking in the direction of the main door and making me wonder if someone was guarding it. But why? Had the rest of the family not understood the plan?

While I was still trying to identify who was standing in the way, the agent leaped forward, going for the attack. I could only watch as two men rolled around the floor. It took me a moment to identify the second. He was Minsheng's friend and our getaway driver from the day before, Chris.

They didn't fight for long, the half-gnome pulling back and getting to his feet. The wrestling on the floor had moved them both away from the door. Rather than continuing to fight, the agent lunged to the door, yanked it open, and ran out into the night.

I rushed after him, desperate not to lose sight of the fleeing man. Zephyr came with me, already in the air. Before I could get out the door, Chris grabbed my arm. More than a little angry at being delayed, I went to use magic to push him away.

"It's okay," he said. "I stuck a tracker on him."

"What do you mean, you stuck a tracker on him?" I demanded, knowing I sounded angrier than I should.

"Minsheng told me the plan. I had a short-distance tracker. Thought that would be easier than having to tail this guy all the way back to HQ. So, you're welcome."

I bit down on my retort, not pleased someone was trying to solve my problems for me. I knew he was just trying to help, but part of me wanted to solve the problem myself. I wanted to go after the agent, and I wanted to be the one who found out where they came from.

Only the knowledge that this was a little petty kept me from bursting out in an angry tirade. Eventually, I nodded. The half-gnome was right; technology could solve this problem better than I could.

No sooner had I thought this than Minsheng appeared. He carried a dark coat, which he held out as soon as he saw me.

"It's cold out there, and this will help you blend in," he explained.

I noticed he also had a bag on his back and a flashlight in one hand. With Zephyr on the ground by my feet, all three of them looked at me.

"All right, let's do this." Without looking back, I opened the door. It was time for us to be the hunters and the agents to be the prey.

CHAPTER TWENTY-ONE

We'd only been out in the cold for a couple of minutes when I felt the first few raindrops. Because it was early evening, Zephyr wasn't flying anymore but sat on my shoulder. He was definitely getting too heavy.

He let out an annoyed rawrl and looked at me.

"Sorry, buddy," I said. "I can't stop the rain."

"It will help cover us," Minsheng said, apparently not bothered by the weather. I sighed. He was right, but I didn't have to like it. Chris held the small tracker unit, the display showing how far ahead of us the agent was.

In my head, I played scenes of us following a sewer pipe all the way out of the city or turning up at a public toilet to find it in a trash can, but so far, so good. When it had been ahead of us for a while, it began to speed up.

Now and then, I'd glanced at the screen over Chris's shoulder, but I stared now, wondering what would happen when it reached the edge. Were we about to lose it? Relief took the tension out of my torso as I watched the map zoom out and show us the moving dot.

After a little while, the agent turned, leading us in a strange pattern. For a moment, I wondered if he was lost or stuck in a one-way system, but it seemed too deliberate.

"Trying to lose a tail," I said, thinking out loud.

"Looks like it. Good thing we got a tracker on him." Minsheng smiled. The gesture looked a little out of place in the rain. It had soaked what little hair he had and flattened it to his head, and the sheen from the waterproof black material of his coat didn't help.

I shuddered at the thought of how I looked. *At least I've got a badass dragon on one shoulder*, I thought. It was some comfort. It didn't make the rain any more pleasant, however.

"Why don't we get a bus?" I asked when we passed a stop. "Or a cab."

"We don't know where he's actually going," Minsheng replied. "The agent hasn't settled on a particular direction yet."

What if he's not going back to the office? I thought, only just stopping myself from asking the question out loud. But he had to report to someone, and agents like him usually reported to someone in an office. Someone who sat behind a desk and had others take the risks, no doubt more cavalier with the lives of others than they had any right to be but getting away with it because that was the way things were.

I sighed as I tried to imagine that person. It was the one behind that desk I needed to talk to. They were the only ones with the power to stop this madness.

Finally, the agent slowed and came to a halt. He'd passed that spot several times, but he was stopping there now. It gave our bedraggled little group some forward momentum, and we hurried through the evening toward his location.

The dot moved around a little more before settling in one place for a while. I was more than a little grateful for the ability to catch up, but thoughts of finding the tracker in a trash can popped into my head again.

Thankfully, we continued to get closer until we saw a large building, its walls glass and steel. Was this the HQ? The dot had stopped inside it.

We found a sheltered position under the awning of a shuttered shop a little farther away, the night helping to hide us in shadows and gloom.

"Here," Chris said, handing me the device. "I'm going to do a tour around the building, see if I can work out if all of it is the agency from the outside."

I nodded, studying the dot. Chris frowned at me for a moment, then pointed at a couple of buttons.

"This first one toggles between vertical view and the horizontal planes, letting you know if the target being tracked is on a different floor or in an airplane. The other button controls the frequency and updates the positioning. It's set to be pretty sensitive right now."

"Great," I replied as the dot moved again for a moment, then making a ninety-degree turn toward us.

"Coming this way," I said. I wanted to warn Minsheng, but he wasn't paying attention for the moment. Instead, he was looking at Chris as the half-gnome hurried away.

"Why don't you go with him?" I suggested. "It's better for us to be in pairs than have one of us alone."

"No," Minsheng said. "You're my ward. My duty is to you."

"Zephyr and I will be all right for a bit, I'm sure. We're not moving from this spot."

Minsheng still shook his head. "If we want more information, we'll have to move."

"Let's order pizza," I said. "Have you got a phone?"

"Why on earth would you want pizza? We had dinner only an hour ago, and we don't want to draw attention to ourselves. Standing here eating pizza is going to draw attention."

"To deliver to the building. Great way to go inside and look innocent. Scope out the lobby, etc."

Minsheng stared at me, his mouth open. Had I just suggested something he'd never even considered? Pulling out his phone, he asked me what I wanted.

"Pepperoni," I said. "With extra cheese...and extra meat."

"So, a meat feast with extra pepperoni and cheese," he said, tapping on the screen. I rolled my eyes, acting like I was annoyed he'd decided to order something different but really grateful. A meat feast sounded awesome, especially given the appetite I had since I'd started moving air about with nothing but the power of my magic.

"You should order some other stuff, like a dessert and a drink so it looks like someone's dinner," I said as he was finishing up. He exhaled, looking as if he might protest, but he didn't, tapping again instead.

The pizza arrived at the building around the corner, Minsheng collecting it as if he'd just come out of the nearby building before bringing it to me. He almost dropped the bottle of soda, but I managed to catch it.

"Hop down, Zephyr," I said as I also took the pizza and the tub of ice cream. The dragon obeyed, but he blinked, no doubt not impressed with being asked to get down onto the wet ground and lose the benefit of my body heat.

"You're not going in there," Minsheng said. "They'll recognize you."

"I'll use a different accent and walk differently. I'm wearing completely different clothes. The receptionist isn't going to know who I am."

As I was speaking, Chris came back. He took one look at the delivery I was holding and grinned.

"Now, that's my kind of improvising," he said, his yellow eyes alight. In the dark, without knowing it was because he was part gnome, I'd have thought the look creepy, but I took it for what it was: amusement and approval of my idea.

Chris reached forward and played with my hair, proving adept at the task.

"There," he said a moment later, having put it into two tails. Then he pulled a packet of gum out of his pocket and offered me a piece. I took it and shoved it in my mouth, chewing it to soften it up.

"Perfect," Chris said, giving me a double thumbs-up.

"Zephyr, wait here. I'll be back in a moment," I said, trying to ignore the painful knotted mess my stomach was now in. I tried to look confident, brusque, and ready to drop off the pizza as I strode inside.

As I'd suspected, there was a receptionist and a set of different company names and floors on a metal plaque by the stairs and elevator. So, the agency didn't occupy the whole building. That was something, at least.

I looked at the names and went up to the receptionist. "Looking for a James Mitchel," I said, making the name up on the fly. "Ordered a meat feast, extra meat. Sounded butch, slightly Texan on the phone."

The receptionist raised her eyebrows for a moment but shook her head.

"No, sorry," she replied. "Don't recognize the name."

As soon as she began uttering her negative, as I knew she would, I wandered back to the company names.

"Anyone on any of these floors? Maybe I could pop up and ask."

"No, sorry, the only ones with people on them are locked off," she said, beginning to get up. I recognized a few of the names and knew they were legit companies, but one company stood out—Mafcca. It was a strange name, and it occupied 2a and 3a, whatever that meant. Given where the dot had stopped, I was pretty sure our agent was on floor three.

"Mafcca," I said. "That rings a bell." I moved toward the stairs as I said it.

"I wouldn't go up unless you're sure," she said, now coming around the desk. "They *really* don't like unexpected visitors."

Something about her voice sounded frightened, and there was no way I was going to get a person who was clearly kind and unaffiliated to the agency in trouble just to scope the place out.

"No worries," I said. "I'll take this back out and stick it in the warm bag again. I can try to phone the boss, see if he can locate the guy for me or narrow it down. Thanks for your help."

As I was turning, she nodded to someone over my shoulder. I moved slower, not sure I wanted to see who it was or let them see me. By the time I'd turned around, I could see I was being ignored by the two agents standing with their sides to me, facing the elevator. One pressed the button several times, clearly impatient.

I walked behind them as the elevator doors opened. The agent on the left took a small, strangely shaped key out of his pocket, putting it into a hole or aperture I couldn't see. Trying not to stare obviously, I hurried toward the front door.

Without looking back, I crossed the road and rejoined my friends. As I got closer to them, I saw Minsheng relax.

"Who wants pizza?" I asked, grinning.

Minsheng didn't look impressed, but his friend dug right in. The rain had eased off a little, but it was still a damp and dreary atmosphere.

"What now?" I asked, handing Zephyr a slice of pizza. "I assume you want to gather some supplies, make a plan, that kind of thing before we go rushing in and attack."

"I think we should discuss it at the very least." Minsheng finally took a slice.

I told them everything I'd learned in my short visit, including the detail about the elevator and what floor I thought they were on. Minsheng frowned when I mentioned the agents who'd come in and how they'd almost seen me. No doubt he wanted to keep me safe, but I'd survived against the agents for several days before Minsheng had helped me. I didn't appreciate being mollycoddled now.

"I found a back way in," Chris said. "Think it was a fire

escape. If it could get us up to another business on floor two or floor three, I could probably cut a way through."

"I don't suppose we can do what they do in the movies, can we?" I asked. "Get a floor plan or something?"

Both my companions chuckled, but before I could assume I *couldn't* get a floor plan, Chris nodded.

"Give me a couple of days."

Minsheng blinked a few times, staring at him.

"What?" the half-gnome asked, shrugging. "I know some people. How do you think I've kept myself alive and made sure I didn't disappear like all the other half-gnomes out there?"

"All right," Minsheng said. "It gives us time to gather supplies, train a bit more, and plan a proper attack."

"Sounds good to me," I replied, grinning.

"I still can't quite believe we're going to do this." Minsheng shook his head.

As I followed Minsheng and Chris back to the restaurant, Zephyr trotting along at my side, I realized I *could* believe we were doing this. Just planning it and going into the building while pretending to be a delivery driver had made a part of me come alive. I was made for this.

CHAPTER TWENTY-TWO

Standing in the dojo, Zephyr beside me and Minsheng wearing all the padded protection possible, I prepared to fight. We'd been training all morning. Part of me felt exhausted, but I also felt alive.

"This time, try to combine your ability to move the air with your normal strikes. You want to use your magic to enhance your normal attacks. If you are always attacking people with just wind, you'll wear yourself out and have nothing left for when you really need it." Minsheng waved me forward.

Ideally, I'd be strong enough to use magic all the time, as Tuviel had. The stories in Minsheng's only English-language book told of her mastering her magic so well that she could power an entire town with nothing but wind. I'd been reading the book a little bit each night before bed. I had just reached a section where they talked about her starting tornadoes, her powers were so advanced.

Last night I'd dreamed of being that powerful. Of swooping down on the agency, riding Zephyr, and making them regret ever trying to hunt me down. I'd woken to a much smaller dragon and much weaker powers. but one day, I was going to be just like Tuviel.

It had made me feel determined. I was going to succeed, and no one was going to stop me.

Holding this thought in mind, I tapped into the raw magic somewhere inside me and used it to speed my attacks. With the karate I had already learned and my newfound ability, I aimed the first strike at Minsheng.

At first Minsheng could keep up, defending himself with blocks and dodges my old sensei would have been proud of. But I was growing faster, learning just how much wind and air I could put behind my strikes to slip them past my Shishou's defenses.

I pummeled him, strike after strike hitting the pads.

"Enough, enough," he said, lifting his hands in surrender.

"Sorry," I replied, guilt making me check if he was all right. For a moment, I had been lost in my desire to defeat the agency and had forgotten I was sparring with my trainer.

"I'm unharmed," he said. "But much longer, and that wouldn't have been true. You're growing stronger. I don't feel any better about you attacking the agency, but you can definitely hold your own in a fight now. No one will be mugging you anytime soon, that's for sure."

I grinned, grateful that he was both unhurt and praising my abilities.

"Let's have lunch, and then this afternoon, we'll teach you and Zephyr to work together better. It shouldn't be long before he learns to talk."

"He'll be able to talk?" I asked. I stopped where I was, feeling like there was still a lot I didn't know—and if it was about my dragon, I wanted to know it right now.

"Yes, any day now. That genetic memory will open up to him. It should make it much easier for the two of you to work together."

"Genetic memory?" I sat down, making it clear I wasn't moving until Minsheng explained. Zephyr came over and sat down as well, his mouth hanging open in a grin.

"It seems I have some explaining to do," Minsheng said as he also sat. "There's a reason most people want to bond with a dragon, and the reason only the most powerful elves are granted the honor. As a dragon matures and develops, becoming an adult, the genetic memory of its ancestors unlocks. This is what is happening with Zephyr, and it will continue to happen for several years."

"All of his ancestors?" I asked, still trying to wrap my head around it. "As in, every dragon that ever lived?"

"Every dragon in his direct line, up until the moment he was born. He'll know everything they knew, including how to talk."

I was stunned. That was a serious advantage. I could see why Minsheng hadn't been worrying about training him to fight. As soon as the memories unlocked, Zephyr was going to know anyway.

"Wait a second," I said, suddenly thinking of something. "Then why did we bother to teach him to fly?"

"Because he needed to know before the memory would have unlocked."

I opened my mouth to object, but the more I thought

about it, the more sense it made. I couldn't carry Zephyr around in a bag much longer. He was getting too heavy.

Satisfied, for now, I got up and we went back to the dining room to have some lunch. Someone had anticipated our desire, and there were several dishes laid out for us to eat.

We were halfway through eating when Chris burst into the room.

"There you are," he said. "I need your help. Right now."

At first I thought he was talking to Minsheng, but then I realized he was looking at me. I raised an eyebrow.

"I need a distraction." As he spoke, he held up an outfit —the skimpy costume of a TV character. One with a dragon. Before I could object, Minsheng did.

"Absolutely no way," my Shishou said, getting to his feet.

"You haven't even heard the plan yet," Chris replied.

"I don't need to. There's no way she's putting herself in danger when she doesn't need to."

"There's no way I'm wearing that, either," I replied.

"It's the only way to get the floor plan."

I frowned, wanting to object again, but Chris sighed and sat down.

"I've only got a few minutes, so I'll try to explain quickly," he said.

Minsheng opened his mouth as if he were going to protest, but Chris held up his hand. "Please, just hear me out. I don't have long."

"Okay, but it had really better be the only way if you're going to get me to wear that dress," I replied.

He quickly explained, making it clear it was by far the best choice.

By the time he'd told me everything, I wouldn't have agreed that it was the only way, but any other method would have taken days. I didn't want to wait that long.

When Chris had finished talking, I sighed. I still didn't like the idea, but it was clear I was going to have to do it.

"All right," I said. "Let's get this over and done with and make it quick."

"You're not seriously considering this?" Minsheng asked.

"He's right; it's the best short-term plan. And I'm tired of hiding. We're not waiting any longer for a different plan to work."

Before Minsheng could say anything else and I could change my mind, I took the dress from Chris and went to get changed.

It took me a while to arrange my hair in a suitable style, but Chris came to help me. Once again showing he was adept at styling female hair, he soon had me sorted.

"How do I look?" I asked when Minsheng appeared in the doorway.

He rolled his eyes before looking at me. "Like a sluttier version of a dragon rider."

"Good. That's the point."

I made my way downstairs, followed by an excited Chris, Zephyr trailing after us. We hurried out to the car, Zephyr and I getting in the back.

To my surprise, Minsheng got in the front, bringing a small bag with him.

"I'll be the backup. In case all this goes wrong," he explained.

"Thanks," I said, truly grateful. I might have been hard on Minsheng a couple of times, but I really did appreciate everything he was doing for me.

It only took ten minutes to get to the drop-off point. I got out of the car, then leaned back in to tuck an arm under Zephyr's midsection and lift him out.

"You need to pretend to be a robot," I said to Zephyr.

The dragon let out a roar, sounding a little different than normal. I wondered if he was trying to say he understood or pretending to be robotic. Either way, Chris was motioning for me to hurry up, and I knew I didn't have long. It was time to be a distraction.

I walked into the nearby building, which in the light of day, I could see was a records office. And almost like last night, I walked up to the reception desk. This time, however, I was asking for someone real.

"Hi," I said, trying to ignore the raised eyebrows and slight frown the receptionist gave me. "I'm looking for Tom Finch."

"I'm not sure anyone by that name works here." She pursed her lips and looked me up and down.

"I know I look a little unconventional, but I'm a birth-day-gram. Someone paid me to come say happy birthday to the guy. I don't get paid if I don't find Tom Finch, wave my robotic dragon at him, sing *Happy Birthday*, and let him take a photo."

"He's on duty, and I'm not sure I should let you."

"I don't wanna get in the way, but I really need the

money. I'm trying to pay my way through medical school. I'll be as quick as I can."

That seemed to do the trick. Whether it was the quick lie about medical school or just needing money, the receptionist caved and unlocked the door for me.

"He's on the fourth floor, second door to the right," she said as I pulled the door open.

"Thank you so much," I enthused. "You're amazing."

I put Zephyr down, my arms already aching from the weight of him. He bounded up the stairs beside me as I hurried toward the right floor, noticing I was a minute or two later than I ought to have been.

By the time I reached the fourth floor, my legs ached. Even Zephyr was panting.

It didn't take me long to find a guard. He was right where the receptionist had said he would be.

"Hi," I said. "Are you Tom Finch?"

For a moment he didn't reply, just staring at me. Then he noticed the dragon.

"Is that real?" he asked. "Is that a real dragon?"

"No, silly, dragons aren't real. He's animatronic." I moved a little closer.

"So...uhh, why are you here?" he asked. "This area isn't open to civilians."

"I'm a birthday-gram," I replied, beaming. "I'm here to sing you *Happy Birthday*."

For a moment I worried that he was going to tell me it wasn't his birthday, but then he grinned.

"I didn't think anyone had remembered," he replied. "Who sent you?"

"I'm not allowed to say. Sorry." I looked around, trying

to see if there was a better room for us to be in. I needed him out of the way for a few minutes.

"Have you got a desk or something?" I asked.

"Don't need one. I just wander these halls, making sure no one gets in. Some of these archives are confidential, protected stuff. I'm supposed to make sure no one takes anything. At least, not without permission."

"Right," I replied. "Is there anywhere off to the side I can put the dragon down?"

The guard looked around, not moving. I tried not to seem panicked, knowing I didn't have long to get him to go somewhere else. But eventually, he nodded.

"This way," he said.

He started walking away, and I could only hope it wasn't in Chris' direction. I followed, Zephyr trotting along the floor beside me. His movements were a little more jerky than normal since he was pretending to be robotic, as we'd discussed.

He opened a door on the left before flicking on the light. Inside was an office, complete with a desk.

"The boss isn't in today. I'm sure he won't mind if we borrow his room for a moment."

"Fantastic," I said, lifting Zephyr up and putting him on the table. "Zephyr, roar."

Zephyr wriggled his bum, padded his feet up and down in a faintly robotic fashion, and let out a small roar.

"Wow," the guard said. "He's really realistic."

"It's amazing what they can do these days." I grinned and stroked the dragon as if it was real. Not hard, given he was, but I had to make it look like I was trying too hard.

"Can I stroke it?" he asked.

"Sure," I replied. It would buy more time. Chris had asked me to give him at least five minutes, something I hadn't thought doable at first, but so far, so good.

The guard reached out and very tentatively stroked Zephyr's head. My dragon managed to keep so still even I couldn't see him moving. It made it look like he was voice-commanded by me. I waited as Tom stroked Zephyr several times, marveling at how that felt.

"It feels so lifelike."

"Really?" I exclaimed. "I've never met anyone who has stroked a real dragon before."

That made Tom chuckle but confirmed that he thought the dragon before him was as much of a joke as what I'd just said.

As soon as stroking Zephyr lost its appeal, I knew I was going to have to do the bit I dreaded most. Sing.

Grinning at him, I burst into the best rendition of *Happy Birthday* I could manage. It was dreadful, but Tom Finch didn't seem to care. He smiled like a Cheshire Cat the whole way through.

Hoping I'd delayed him for at least five minutes, I picked up Zephyr again.

"Well, I'm done," I said. "I hope you have a good birthday."

"Just working and then going home." He got the door for me, thankfully not used to this sort of thing enough to think he should get a photo. "I'll grab takeaway and maybe some cake on the way."

I pouted, doing my best Marilyn Monroe impression at how sad that sounded. About to leave, I noticed someone running through the door beyond us. Buying him a fraction more time, I lifted up onto the tips of my toes and kissed Tom on the cheek.

"Goodbye," I said as I walked away. As soon as I was through the door and out of sight, I put Zephyr down.

Hoping Chris had gotten what we needed, I hurried back downstairs.

"Completely made his day," I said as I went past the reception desk.

"Didn't even know it was his birthday," she replied.

"Get him a cake if you can. Even just a little one. He said he wasn't going to get one."

"Oh, the poor guy. I know just the bakery. They'll even put little candles on it."

I waved as I hurried out the main door, feeling like I'd done my good deed for the day as well as helped get the plans. It sounded like I'd given a sad, lonely man one of his best birthdays ever.

Minsheng was still waiting in the car two blocks away. He opened the back door for me as I came closer. No sooner had I put Zephyr in and climbed in myself than Chris appeared, carrying a tube. The kind that normally held a poster.

He was humming a tune and looked more than a little pleased with himself.

"Did you get it?" I asked, barely letting him get in the car first.

"Got it," he replied as he handed the tube to Minsheng.

I sighed. It was becoming a real plan.

CHAPTER TWENTY-THREE

Sitting around the dining room table at Minsheng's restaurant, Minsheng, Chris, and I pored over the plans for the agency building.

"This is where the receptionist is," I said, pointing at a small section on the bottom floor of the blueprint. "There's the elevator shaft and the stairwell."

"And you said they were on floor two and three?" Chris asked.

I nodded, pointing at the only two parts of those floors where the agency could be. It occupied about a third of two different floors, nowhere near as big as it had looked from the outside.

"I think we should go into the building in two teams," I said. "Zephyr and I will go up in the elevator."

"We don't have a key," Minsheng pointed out.

"No. I'm going to mug one of the agents on the way in."

"And just waltz up the elevator?" Minsheng asked. He frowned, no doubt displeased with my choice of entry.

"No one's going to shoot me. If they were going to do

that, they'd have done it already. I'm the person they want, remember?"

"And while she's distracting them at the front door, we can be going in through the back," Chris added.

"There isn't a back door."

"We're going to make one." Chris grinned.

"How long do you think it will take you to get in and get through?" I asked. "So I know how long it'll be until the cavalry arrives."

"About ten minutes, maybe a minute or two more."

I nodded. I could just about handle that. With all the training I'd recently gotten, I was pretty sure I could buffet any darts away. I'd take the adrenaline shot I'd stolen from a previous agent with me just in case.

"I'm going to need to source some equipment." Chris stood up. "I should be back a little before nightfall."

"There's a couple of things I'd like you to get for me too," I said. I reached for a piece of scrap paper and jotted down what I'd need. A bug and a transceiver, one that worked long distance and would record when I couldn't listen, plus better shoes. The ones I was wearing had no grip, and I was going to need it.

Chris took one look at my list and nodded. Without another word, he left.

"Can you teach me and Zephyr how to fight better together?" I asked, looking at Minsheng.

After rolling up the map, he nodded.

"Come on then," he replied. "To the training room."

I followed him, grabbing a couple of cookies from the plate on the sideboard before I did. If I was going to be doing lots of magic later, I needed to make sure I had plenty of energy.

We were soon down in the training room, standing in the one area of the room I hadn't used yet. The space had been made up like a mock office or part of a building, with shorter than normal walls. There were plenty of twists and turns, corners, and hallways from where people could jump out at me.

"Think of this as an assault course," Minsheng explained. "Try to get from one end to the other without getting hit *and* take out every guard along the way."

"Guard?" I asked, not sure what he meant.

"You'll see what I mean."

Before I could ask any other questions, Minsheng disappeared around a wall.

"Looks like it's just you and me, Zephyr," I said. I looked down at him. He bounced from one front paw to the other and opened his mouth in a grin.

"Come on, then." I began jogging down the first corridor. As I went around the next corner, Zephyr still at my side, a cardboard cutout of a man sprang out of the wall.

I slid to a halt as Zephyr leaped up and smacked into its stomach area with his front paws. He rebounded off, flapping his wings as the cutout slid back into the wall. There was a little ping went somewhere.

Assuming that meant I'd defeated that obstacle, I kept going. Expecting more cardboard people, I was a little more wary, exchanging speed for care.

As I came round the next corner, there was an open doorway. Coming closer, I drew on some of the magic inside me. This time when a silhouette flew at me, I was ready. A blast of air hit it in the chest.

The target had barely swung open when it flew back, disappearing from sight and setting off another little ping. Grinning at our success so far, Zephyr and I kept going.

We moved through the entire obstacle course, taking out the bad guys and earning ourselves a little mark of recognition each time. A couple of times they surprised me, coming down from the ceiling or up from the floor, but Zephyr had my back, seeming to know exactly where to be and breathing gas on a couple of them. Somehow the cardboard cutouts were sophisticated enough to detect that.

I got to the end to find Minsheng standing there with a stopwatch. He stopped it as I stepped over the line and Zephyr landed.

"Twenty-two minutes and thirty-five seconds," he said. "Not too bad for your first attempt."

"Want me to do it again?" I asked, feeling good.

For a moment I thought Minsheng was going to say no, but after a pause, he nodded.

"See if you can do it faster, but don't miss a target. You get a minute penalty for every one you don't vanquish."

Taking a deep breath and trying to calm my racing heart back down, I prepared to go through again. I glanced at Zephyr, checking he was also ready.

He let out a little roar and raced ahead. I chuckled as I ran after him. Someone was raring to go.

Zephyr did the same move on the first guard, then launched himself into the air to fly around the rest of the maze. I hurried to keep up, taking out as many of the cardboard cutout guards as I could along the way.

Our second run-through was a couple of minutes quicker, but we must have missed one target.

"Even with the minute penalty, we're still quicker," I said, pouting.

Minsheng chuckled before speaking, "If it was a real-life situation, however, you'd have someone sneak-attack you from behind."

"But I was so fast he wouldn't have caught me," I said, folding my arms across my chest.

Minsheng opened his mouth before closing it again.

"Why don't you try it again?" he eventually asked.

I rolled my eyes but did as he suggested. The training would be good for me, especially as I didn't know for sure what I would have to face later that night.

We trained for the rest of the afternoon, and by the end, I'd managed to shave another three minutes off my time. I'd also gotten better at using a combination of martial arts and magic, using air to make my attacks faster and more powerful.

"There's still plenty to work on," Minsheng said. "But for now, that will do."

I grinned, feeling more than a little smug.

We made our way back to the normal dining room. This time we were a little early. Daisy was still cooking, the smells from the kitchen heavenly. I began setting the table and making myself useful. It was the least I could do for all the wonderful cooking they'd done for me and the way they'd taken me in.

Chris arrived just as dinner was being placed on the table. Flicking me a wink, he sat down with the rest of us.

I ate dinner as fast as I could. Not only did I want to see what Chris had brought with him, but I was also desperate to get on with the plan.

Thankfully, Minsheng and Chris were of similar minds. Within fifteen minutes, we were all done and heading up to the bedrooms to prepare for what came next.

It seemed Chris had snuck up before dinner since there was an array of different tech sitting on my bedroom floor, and a new pair of sneakers, too. I wasn't sure how I felt about him going in my room when I wasn't there, but I was more than a little distracted by all the shiny.

"This is for you," he said, handing me a small box.

"The bug and receiver?" I asked, looking at it. He nodded, already moving onto the next piece of gear.

I placed it on the bed and began adding everything else I thought I'd need. There was the adrenaline shot, a flash-light, the night-vision goggles Chris had given me the night before, and the gun and darts I'd stolen from an agent several days ago. Now I just needed a pair of pants that could hold it all.

It was the age-old problem of a woman—finding a pair of pants with enough pockets.

As I surveyed all my gear, Minsheng appeared. He'd anticipated my problem and carried a pair of men's cargo pants, size small.

"Perfect," I said, beaming at him. "Give me a moment to get changed."

I hurried into the bathroom, definitely not letting them

see me get dressed. It didn't take long. The pants were a little baggy around the waist but fit otherwise.

As soon as they were on, I went back to my bedroom and started loading up the pockets. I stuck the gun on the right-hand side, where I would be able to grab it in a fight without much trouble.

With that done, I looked at Zephyr. There wasn't a lot he could do to prepare, but I felt like he ought to do something. He merely blinked at me, however, ready and waiting for whatever followed.

I moved on to Chris and Minsheng. Both of them were still loading their pockets. I watched as they added a similar variety of things: flashlights, night-vision goggles and a few other tools I didn't recognize. Finally, Chris grabbed a small backpack and loaded it with a rope, some canteens, glow sticks, and snack bars.

"Well, you look prepared." I came closer, as ready as I was ever going to be. "Let's get this show on the road."

Neither of them argued, and we headed out to the car.

We didn't stop at the same location as the day before, instead leaving the car three or four blocks away. We walked the rest of the way, stopping in the dark behind a bush, just able to see the entrance of the agency building.

"Let me guess, now we wait?" I asked.

"Pretty much," Chris replied.

I sighed. I hated waiting. Didn't everyone?

Crouched beside Zephyr, I stroked him absentmindedly. I had a feeling this was going to be a long evening.

Two hours passed, and there was no sign of another agent. My feet hurt, and I was more than a little bored. Although we'd rotated taking turns with the night-vision goggles watching the front door of the agency building, it was mundane work, and I couldn't stand it any longer.

"Why don't we draw an agent out?" I asked. "Make them think they found me somewhere else."

"I'm not sure I like that idea," Minsheng replied.

"Do you have a better one?" I asked, putting my hands on my hips.

After a moment, Minsheng shook his head. "No. It's better than anything I came up with. But how are we going to make them think they found you somewhere else?"

"By being somewhere else. Briefly. Just need a tourist to take a photo of Zephyr."

"Where are you going to find a tourist at this time of night?"

"Well, aren't you Mr. Twenty Questions? I just need a packed bar or a busker or something."

"If we use the car to drop you off somewhere and pick you up ten minutes later, do you think that will be long enough?" Chris asked.

I thought about it for a moment, tilting my head to the side. Eventually, I nodded.

More than a little relieved to be doing something, we hurried back to the car, leaving Minsheng to watch the agency door. He was under strict instructions to text us if he saw any activity.

Chris had no idea where to go, so I directed him to a place near my old apartment. There was a great rock 'n roll bar there.

He dropped me off around the corner, and I took Zephyr with me. I didn't let him fly, not wanting to make it obvious he was a real dragon. I wanted people to be able to doubt they'd seen him afterward. To claim it was an automaton, as I had earlier, or some other bizarre alternative.

It didn't take us long to get to the bar. I wasn't dressed for the place, but they let me in, although the man on the door eyed Zephyr warily.

Picking up the dragon, I helped him onto my shoulder. He didn't completely fit anymore, but it was better than leaving him on the floor. The place was hopping, and I didn't want him to get trampled.

Together, we went up to the bar. At first, no one seemed to notice us. Not until the bartender did. He looked my way, his mouth falling open when he noticed Zephyr.

"Can I get a Coke?" I asked, slapping a bill on the counter. The bartender continued to stare.

"Is that real?" he asked, his question drawing the attention of people nearby.

"Yes, but it's okay. He doesn't breathe fire."

The people around me must've heard what I said because a ripple of silence moved out from us. It was followed by a wave of whispers, people talking in hushed tones to the person next to them as they tried to work out what was on my shoulder.

The bartender still didn't get me a drink. I stared at him for a moment, not sure what to do.

"Can I get that drink, please?" I asked.

"Oh," he finally replied. "Of course. Just give me a moment."

He put the Coke can down on the counter and went back to staring at the dragon.

"Does he want a drink as well?" he asked.

I shook my head, struggling not to laugh. It was clear no one knew how to act around a dragon. I supposed I hadn't known either, but I'd had a little while to adjust.

"Is it really real?" the woman beside me asked. Again, I nodded.

"Can I touch it?"

"You can stroke him as long as you're careful." I turned slightly, making it easier for her to reach him. Zephyr, once again understanding what was going on, slowly lowered his head, leaning toward her hand.

That made her brave, and she touched her fingers to the top of his head and ran them down his back. As she did, a grin broke out on her face.

"There. Not so scary, huh?" I asked.

That seemed to make others bolder as well. Out of the corner of my eye, I noticed someone get their phone out and take a photo. That was enough. I didn't doubt the agency would be monitoring every social media app in existence. I also knew that was where my photographer would put it within seconds. Who wouldn't? He'd just seen a dragon for the first time.

"Thanks for the drink," I said as I picked up my can and left, the crowd parting before me.

I found Chris waiting right where I'd left him, and I felt a sense of relief. I hadn't realized how tense I'd been until I wasn't anymore.

As soon as I was inside the car, Zephyr jumped off my shoulders onto the seat beside me. For a moment my shoulders ached, the dragon far too heavy to be carried like that for even a few minutes.

"Minsheng's just texted," Chris said as he pulled away. "It worked. There's agents on the way."

I grinned. They'd investigate, and of course, they wouldn't find me. When they returned to their office to make a full report, I would be able to follow them inside.

CHAPTER TWENTY-FOUR

Despite knowing the agents wouldn't find me, we waited for another hour for them to return. By then it was almost midnight, and I was frozen.

"Come on. How long does it take to work out that I'm not there anymore?" I stomped my feet, trying to get some life back into them.

"Quiet," Minsheng said, taking his turn watching the door. "They're back."

"Then wish me luck," I replied as I walked out from behind the bush. Zephyr followed me automatically, knowing we were about to go into action.

While we'd waited, I hadn't felt that nervous. But now that it was happening, nervous thoughts flooded my mind. As my heart began to race, and my stomach knotted. What if there were more agents than I could cope with?

I pushed the thoughts away and kept walking. I had to do this. It was time they left me alone.

I wasn't far behind the agents when they reached the door, but I had to sprint the last few yards. They were only just inside when I caught up to them. I grabbed the closest agent's wrist as he swung it back in his stride. Spinning, I used my momentum to turn him around and land him on his back. Immediately, Zephyr exhaled at his face.

The gas had him paralyzed in seconds.

I turned to the second agent as the receptionist got to her feet. The agent was pulling his gun, but I kicked up. My foot connected with the weapon, sending it flying.

"Why, you little—"

I lunged forward with a right hook, using an extra blast of wind to make the move more powerful. It caught him in the stomach. Letting out an *oof*, he crumpled.

Bringing my elbow down on his shoulder blade, I sent him crashing to the floor. Before he could recover, Zephyr had breathed on him as well. I patted him down, looking for the key I needed. He didn't have it.

"Damn," I said as I went over to the first one. I patted him down as well.

"Hey," the receptionist said, getting my attention. "You're the girl from yesterday."

"Yes. I am. And yes, the dragon is real. Sorry about that."

She nodded, staring at Zephyr as she backed toward her desk. I saw her hand reaching for something.

"I don't want to hurt you. In fact, I don't want to hurt anyone. You see, I found this dragon a few days ago. Like you, I didn't believe they existed, but it's clear they do. The agency here, with agents like these guys—" I stopped to point at the paralyzed men at my feet, "—are trying to take the dragon and disappear him. I just don't want them to do that. I can't explain it very well, but he sort of bonded to me. I think that makes me his mother somehow, so I'm trying to do what any mother would and keep him safe. That's all. I'm going upstairs to have a word with whoever is in charge. Is that okay with you?"

For a moment I thought the receptionist was going to alert someone anyway, but she looked at Zephyr and then at me and moved away from the desk again. Then she reached into a pocket and pulled out the key I needed.

"Here," she said. "That's the most heartfelt thing anyone's ever said to me. You keep your dragon safe now."

"Thank you," I replied. I hurried toward the elevator, pressing the button to call it down.

I glanced at the receptionist to see her going back to the desk.

"I'm going to have to press the button at some point," she replied.

"Tell them the dragon breathed on you too," I suggested. "But you had the sense to not inhale as much. You can tell them I took the key off you."

She nodded as the elevator doors opened. I hurried inside, Zephyr coming with me.

"Here we go," I said, looking at Zephyr. "Let's teach those agents a lesson."

I put the key in the strangely shaped hole and turned it. A button marked 2a lit up. Without hesitating, I pressed it.

The elevator lurched to life, carrying me upward. Knowing I didn't have long, I sucked up as much energy as I could, drawing the air in around me.

When I arrived, I spotted at least four agents, guns trained on the opening elevator doors. Their mouths fell open as they saw me.

Not about to give them time to react, I unleashed all the

power I'd been gathering. A blast of air flew out from me and hit every one of them, knocking them off their feet.

I rushed forward, Zephyr launching into the air beside me. I didn't know if their guns had darts or not so I left them on the floor where they'd fallen. Instead, I grabbed the one from my pocket, and I shot the prone agents farthest away from me.

While I did that, Zephyr flew to the nearest agent and exhaled. Once more, his cloud of gas ensured an agent wouldn't be getting to his feet anytime soon. I grinned. Four agents already down up here, but I didn't know how many more were in the building.

As four more agents appeared, running from some-where else in the office, I backed through the nearest door-way, ducking as Zephyr followed, still flying. I found myself in a small kitchen, and the smell of coffee and donuts that were beginning to go stale hit me.

Pulling a face, I noticed an array of mugs on the shelves. As the first agent came around the corner, his gun out to shoot, I hit him in the chest with a mug, the blast of wind required to do so sending a tranquilizer dart off-course at the same time.

It didn't stop the agent, but it distracted him long enough that I could hurl another mug at him, this one with my hands as Zephyr banked and came around. As soon as the dragon spotted the agent, he exhaled. A noxious cloud formed around the agent's head.

Not wanting to be boxed in, I ran at the agent. His body paralyzed, we fell into the corridor. On the way out, we caught another agent, knocking him off his feet too.

Before he could get up, I lashed out at him. He caught

my fist, reacting faster than I could. With a sharp twist, he put me in a lock.

Before the agent could do anything else, Zephyr appeared.

"Nice timing," I said as Zephyr breathed out and paralyzed the agent holding me. As the agent went stiff, so did his lock on my wrist. I grunted as I tried to pull my hand free. Two more agents were aiming their guns at me.

"Stop right there," one of the agents said.

I looked at him. Were they really that stupid? Outwardly, I didn't move, but inwardly, I did all the magic I could, sucking in air and preparing to blast it back out.

As the agents advanced, I let it go. It barreled into both of them, sending them flying so far backward they hit the wall with a thud, both of them unconscious.

With only Zephyr for company, I had the time to try to wriggle out of the paralyzed agent's grasp. It rubbed my wrist raw, but eventually, I was free. I hurried forward, looking for an office that appeared more important.

At first all I passed were more cubes, a desk in each with a switched-off computer on top of each one. There were no more agents, or they were hiding.

No doubt getting tired, Zephyr landed. He stayed close to my side, and I held the gun outstretched, at least three more darts left in it.

Before I could get any farther, I heard a thud from the office to my right. I moved cautiously toward the office, pulled open the door, and saw Chris and Minsheng. An agent had his gun trained on Minsheng, who had come in through a hole in the wall.

Without hesitating, I shot the agent in the back. It took

him a moment to fall down, but as he did, Minsheng and Chris rushed forward.

"Took you guys long enough," I said, smiling nonetheless. "I've taken care of most of the agents already."

"The offices on the other side weren't as empty as we thought they'd be," Minsheng replied. "I'm glad to see you're all right, though."

Before any of us could say more, I heard the sound of running feet behind me. I hurried out into the corridor again to see yet another set of four agents rushing our way from the elevator. They were the four Zephyr had already paralyzed. His breath weapon must wear off pretty quickly. I shot two of them, taking them back out again.

The other two had quicker reflexes, both of them darting into open doorways so I couldn't shoot. Not that I had any darts left anyway.

"We'll take care of them," Minsheng said, beckoning for Chris to follow him.

I hesitated, not sure how to tell him to be careful. Now that I'd gained an ally, I didn't want to lose him. I also had a lot of questions still, ones I was pretty sure only he could answer.

But right now we had a job to do, and it was clear I couldn't do it alone. With no more darts, I tucked the gun back into a pocket and went over to the nearest agent. I patted him down, hoping to find more tranquilizer darts.

I was out of luck. All I found were bullets. Frowning and realizing some of them had been aiming loaded guns at me, I kept searching for agents. The building seemed eerily quiet ahead of me, the sounds of fighting fading somewhere behind me.

It took all my self-control not to run back and help Minsheng and Chris, but the sooner I got to whoever was in charge, the sooner I could end this.

As I went around the next corner, I spotted six more agents. They'd formed a sort of shield around an office door, all of them pointing guns my way.

They opened fire as I hit the deck. My reflexes saved me from a barrage of bullets. I rolled as I drew air toward me and looked at Zephyr. The dragon had darted into the air and dived back around the corner.

Knowing he was safe, I concentrated on my magic. I pushed a wave of air out as I got up. From then on, I drew air in with one hand, and with the other hand, I pushed air out. The bullets bent around the wave of air I threw forward. Not daring to run but feeling my powers begin to drain me, I hurried forward.

The agents' mouths fell open as they realized their bullets were having no effect. As I came closer, they stopped shooting altogether.

As soon as they did, I jettisoned all the air I had left at them. Hearing Zephyr roar behind me as the agents stumbled under my barrage, I sprinted at the nearest one. With nothing left but my martial arts, I kicked out.

Still disoriented, he blocked too late, and I caught him in the stomach. I followed it with a spinning back kick, sending him sprawling onto his front. By then Zephyr had caught up, and he exhaled, taking another agent out of the equation.

The other four agents had recovered. As one, they came at me. I drew more air in and blasted it out in a circle. The effect bought me some time, making it hard for the agents to get to me, but I knew I couldn't keep it up.

I hurled myself at another agent, taking us both down. I thumped and thumped whatever part of him my fists could reach. I hadn't come this far to lose at the end.

"Don't shoot her," I heard someone yell from behind. "The boss wants her alive."

I kept punching, the agent beneath me still moving, oblivious to everything else around me. As the agent went still, an arm wrapped around my waist and pulled me backward. I grabbed it, twisting and twirling around at the same time.

Although I tried to make my moves faster by pulling the air around me, my ability to manipulate the element was drained. But despite the lack of extra help, I was still fast, my training paying off. I turned the agent in circles, knocking him off his feet. Before I could do anything else, another agent grabbed me.

Beginning to feel like I was bouncing from agent to agent, I blocked what I could and looked for an opening to attack. To my relief, Minsheng and Chris came running around the corner.

They both pulled out the dart guns and began shooting. Tranquilizers flew through the air. I felt a sting as one hit me, but it hadn't come from Chris or Minsheng.

Another of the agents had had the presence of mind to draw his tranquilizer gun. Once again grateful for my ability to process the sedative quicker, I pulled the dart out and kept fighting.

I could feel the sedative spreading through my system, slowing my reaction times and making it harder to fight.

As two more of the agents fell down, tranquilized, I felt the sting of another dart.

Shitsticks, I thought as I felt my body giving way. I tried to remember where I'd stuck the adrenaline shot as my hands reached for my pockets. Everything around me was a blur. Zephyr's scales flew past while I groped.

My hands finally closed on the small plastic cylinder, and I pulled it out as Minsheng and Chris rushed up. I had no time to wonder what had happened to the other agents before Minsheng took the shot out of my hand and prepared it. Just as he'd done several days earlier, he brought me back from the brink of blackness, jabbing the shot into my thigh and injecting it.

Almost instantly, the world came back into focus. I looked around. All the agents were down, Zephyr was standing by my side, and Minsheng and Chris were standing over me. Minsheng helped me to my feet, and I gave him a small smile.

"Thanks," I said, looking at the final room. The agents had been guarding it, which meant someone important was inside.

CHAPTER TWENTY-FIVE

Once I'd helped Chris and Minsheng tie up all the agents we'd knocked out or paralyzed, I sighed. No one had emerged from the end office yet. Zephyr had been keeping an eye on it the whole time.

"I think I need to do this next bit alone," I said to Minsheng and Chris as I handed Chris the spare zip ties I had. "Well, Zephyr and I need to do it."

I'd expected Minsheng to object, but he nodded and gave Chris a look as the latter tried to respond. Instead, the half-gnome techie shut his mouth again and got out of my way.

After making sure my gun was loaded with more darts and I had the bug I'd been given by Chris in an easy-to-reach pocket, I hurried to the door. There I paused, looking at Zephyr, with my hand on the doorknob.

A moment later, he gave me a slight nod. I turned the knob and pushed the door open as I raised the gun. There was only one person in front of me.

I'd expected to find an older, graying man, perhaps with

glasses, sitting behind a desk, wearing a suit that was a shade of gray to set him apart from all the agents wearing black.

Instead, I found a fairly short woman wearing a plum suit. As soon as she saw me, she shut her laptop and pushed back from the desk, her wheeled chair rolling a foot.

While she got up, she took off her reading glasses and put them on the desk. That was about the only thing I'd gotten right. I kept the gun on her as I strode inside, Zephyr coming too and jumping up onto her desk.

Two large plants sat in each of the far corners of the room, real but watered by a timer pump stuck in the large pot each was planted in.

Perfect, I thought, but I fixed my eyes on the woman. She barely blinked, appearing completely calm.

For a moment no one moved or said anything, until I reached a hand behind me and blasted the door with some air to shut it. It slammed with a loud bang that made her jump.

"I assume you already know who we are," I started, not sure what to say now that I was here but determined that I'd steer the conversation, not her.

"It's Aella-Faye, isn't it?" she asked, perching on the side of the desk as if there wasn't a ten-pound dragon standing on it.

"Yes, and this is Zephyr. Zephyr and I have bonded, which means he belongs to me now. I don't know who the egg belonged to or why I found it where I did, but he's mine now, got it?"

"I know you think he's yours. And I'm aware the little mentor you've—"

"No," I interrupted. "You're not hearing me. Zephyr, I, and my mentor have just taken out your entire office of agents and any more who arrived at the wrong moment. There's nothing stopping me from ending your life or theirs, but I don't want violence. I don't want conflict. All I want to do is go raise my dragon and live the closest thing we can to a normal life. And that's all he wants. I don't *think* he's mine. I *know* he's mine, understand?"

As if to emphasize my statement, Zephyr jumped down from the desk and came to stand beside me, then roared so loudly it made my ears ring. For a moment I thought I had been deafened, and even Miss Keeping-her-cool widened her eyes.

"I can't let you do that. My agency exists to stop the things the everyday person thinks are mythical from shattering that illusion. Its sole purpose is preventing that."

"You're not hearing me," I replied, growling the words as I took a step forward. "Your agency doesn't exist anymore. Or at least, I could have made sure it didn't. The only reason it does—still—is because I have allowed it. If you don't leave us alone, I *will* end your agency."

As I spoke, I half-concentrated on the bug in my pocket. Although I was tired, I had just about enough energy to slowly lift the tiny object out and very carefully move it to the farthest potted plant.

To keep her focus on me while I did so, I shifted my grip on the gun and took another step forward. It was aimed at her chest now, and she glanced at it.

"So, what, you'll shoot me if you don't get your way?" she asked.

"In the future, maybe," I replied, rolling my eyes as I

slipped the bug around the back of the desk and over toward the plant. "But not today. I've already defeated you today. But I'm not leaving here 'til you assure me you're going to leave us alone."

"Do you think I can do that?"

"Yes. You might not think you can, or it might not have occurred to you that you can, but you're going to. I don't care what you tell whoever you report to. Whether you tell them anything, or you tell them a lie. Because I know you report to someone. You were probably doing so as I walked in. But this ends here. And I won't ask again."

"You haven't said much to convince me. I can bring in more agents."

"Maybe you can, but I defeated all of these with a three-day-old dragon after four training sessions. How long is it going to take you to get new agents? Two days? A week? By then, we'll be stronger. I'm not going to stop training him, and I'm not going to stop strengthening my magic. We'll do whatever we need to protect ourselves."

I slowly lowered the gun, keeping my gaze fixed on her as my mind placed the bug just behind the plant's pot. I wagered those pots were so heavy that no one was going to be moving them anytime soon.

She blinked a few times, seeming surprised I was no longer aiming the gun at her. I walked to the door, Zephyr following me.

"Come on," I called over my shoulder as I opened the door. "Let me show you where your agents are."

As I walked toward the small restroom Chris and Minsheng had dragged all of the unconscious agents into, I glanced behind me a couple of times. Miss Cool followed, although she did so at a distance.

When she set eyes on her agents, some of them now awake, her mouth fell open.

"Sorry, boss," one of them said. "They took us by surprise."

"And she's got some pretty funky magic powers," another added.

"I see," she replied, looking at me.

"So, do we have a deal?" I asked. "You leave me alone, and I let your agency continue to exist."

"You won't interfere in anything else we do?" she asked.

I shrugged.

"I doubt I'll need to, but I can't promise. I *can* promise not to seek your agents out and to keep a low profile myself. I doubt the world is ready to know dragons exist just yet. I just want to protect this dragon and raise him in safety. He came to me, and I'm some kind of mother now. Mothers do whatever it takes to protect their babies, and I'm doing no less."

She narrowed her eyes, a strange gleam in them as she studied me. I wondered if I should say anything else or promise not to get involved, but I knew I couldn't do that. I had a feeling that at some point, I would get very involved again.

"All right," she said after a pause. "You have your deal, and everyone here will witness it. We'll leave you alone, and you leave us alone."

I nodded, not intending to thank her. Motioning to Minsheng and Chris to leave first, I waited until they were far from harm, then I followed.

"You're going to need to fix the wall in the second office," Chris called over his shoulder.

I struggled not to chuckle as Miss Cool followed me, still keeping her distance. As we waited for the elevator to arrive and take us back downstairs, I took one last look at her.

For a moment I thought I could see fear in her eyes, but then she swallowed it back down, and once again, she appeared calm.

"Perhaps we'll meet again one day," she said. "If we do, it's going to be on very different terms."

"You can be very sure of it," I replied. "My gun won't just have darts in it."

Neither of us got to say anything more since the elevator doors closed and the elevator carried my friends and me down to the bottom floor. I sighed with relief. For now, it was over.

As soon as we reached the first floor, Chris and Minsheng hurried toward the front door. I glanced at the receptionist, seeing her still sitting behind her desk. Our eyes met, and I knew I couldn't leave yet.

"I'll catch up with you," I said.

Minsheng glanced at the receptionist, no doubt taking in her pale face before he nodded. I watched the two men leave before I went over to her.

"Are you okay?" I asked.

"I think so. I haven't been fired, but I must confess, I didn't expect to see you again."

"I'm stronger than I look or, well...faster." I grinned. "And having a dragon helps."

She chuckled, but it was more a reflex than genuine mirth.

"I'm glad I didn't get you fired. Hopefully everything will go back to normal here now."

Exchanging quick smiles by way of goodbye, we parted. Zephyr followed me out of the building, and we hurried toward our rendezvous point.

Within seconds, I was back inside the car and pulling out my transceiver. It was already recording data, and I played it from the beginning.

"Sorry, sir," I heard Miss Cool say. "One of the agents returned to inform me the threat had been neutralized."

"Neutralized?" a deep male voice asked.

"Yes, sir," she replied. "She tried to dive out a window to get away and fell. Clearly thought her elemental magic would save her. The dragon tried to help her. They both hit the ground, and while still groggy, were hit by a car. They're dead."

"It sounds like you've got quite the mess to clean up."

"Thankfully not. The driver sped off moments after. There were no other witnesses."

"Good. You got lucky today, Crawley. Any other mistakes, and I'll have to insist on a full review. This took far too long to contain."

"Understood, sir. It won't happen again, sir."

I grinned as I sat back. We'd done it. Between the four of us, we'd stopped the agents from coming after us.

Minsheng gave me a smile, making it clear he'd listened to the conversation as well.

No one spoke or moved until we were back at the restaurant.

"I think we could all do with some rest," Minsheng said as we went inside, but it was soon clear we weren't going to get the chance yet.

All of his family were waiting up for us. Most of them sat in the dining room, a half-empty bowl of snacks in the middle of the table.

They all began talking at once, no single question distinguishable from another.

"Whoa," Minsheng said, lifting his hands and motioning for them to slow down a bit.

They slowly quieted.

"What happened?" Minsheng's sister asked.

"We're going to be left alone," I replied. "I got the agency commander to agree to leave us alone as long as we don't go public about having a dragon."

"You're going to have to give us more details than that," the chef replied.

It took the best part of an hour for us to tell our stories. At first, I stuttered and stammered over my part of it. Somehow I reached the end of my tale, and Chris took over, telling his part.

"Minsheng and I made our way up to the adjacent office. Nice, quiet little office, or so we thought. There's a late-night worker who needed more of a social life and is gonna wake up in a couple of hours with a really sore head."

That earned Chris some chuckles. He told his story until the point where they'd met up with me.

As soon as we were done talking, many of our audience got up. I assumed they were going to bed, but none of them went right away. Taking me by surprise, they hugged me one by one.

"We all knew you were special. I hope you feel at home here and know you have a new family," Daisy said. "And next time, I want in on your adventures."

I nodded, not trusting my voice. If I said anything, I was pretty sure I was going to cry.

Over the next few minutes, they all left and went to their beds, Chris taking the guest room. After a while, it was just me, Zephyr, and Minsheng.

"I must admit I was very worried about you today, but you were amazing. I don't know what you promised her, but I'm glad I listened to you and we went." Minsheng hugged me. "You should get some rest. We need to plan out a new training room in the morning. One with more room for Zephyr to grow."

"Hear that, Zephyr?" I asked. "We're going to learn all kinds of cool things."

Zephyr let out a happy-sounding rawrl and flapped his wings a few times before folding them back up and coming to sit by my feet.

I watched Minsheng go to bed before I grabbed a handful of the snacks and made my own way upstairs, exhausted. As I shut myself and Zephyr into our room, I sighed.

The furniture, the large bed, the few possessions I'd managed to leave my apartment with, and the cushioned area for Zephyr didn't quite feel like home yet, but they did finally feel like mine.

EPILOGUE

Looking out at the moonlit beach, I checked for signs of strangers. Thankfully, there were no footprints in the sand, and I couldn't see any shadows up ahead.

"Come on, Zephyr," I said, walking forward. "It's safe."

The month-old dragon got out of the car, barely fitting through the door. As soon as he was out, he unfurled his wings and leaped into the air. I reached out, motioned upward, and gave him an extra little lift.

And then I watched, keeping an eye out as he got some exercise. It was three in the morning, the quietest time on the beach and the only time I dared let him get some fresh air.

It wasn't ideal, but it was a routine we'd fallen into as Zephyr had grown. The organization was still working on finding us a warehouse or a similar building that could be used as a better training facility, but it wasn't easy finding anywhere big enough for Zephyr long-term.

Minsheng appeared beside me, yawning. Together we

watched the dark shadow in the sky that was Zephyr flying.

"How much do you think he weighs now?" I asked.

"No idea, but my sister complained that he's eaten us out of beef jerky again."

I chuckled, not surprised. It was his new favorite snack.

"You know, I finally got some info back from the organization today," Minsheng said a few minutes later.

"Anything interesting?" I asked.

"Zephyr's DNA results. He's descended from Azargad. A stronger link than you, but not by much. And also descended from another dragon, which the organization says isn't in the database."

"Is that bad?" I looked at Minsheng, a strange tingle running up my spine.

"No. If anything, it's a good thing. It means more dragons survived than we thought. Perhaps even more have come here from their dimension. Who knows? Whoever his ancestors are, they're powerful."

I nodded, not sure how to process the new information. Minsheng had taught me many more things about the mythical world and everything I'd thought to be part of stories, but I still didn't understand it all.

"That wasn't the only thing I learned. I looked into that building you said you found the egg in to see if I could find out who put it there. It seems to be some kind of warehouse and appears to have been forgotten. It was built and never used, declared off-limits and unsafe, then almost hidden. It was like it was buried, and all paperwork and records that referred to it kept going missing. Can't even find out who owns the thing."

I opened my mouth to ask a question, but a strange light in Minsheng's eyes stopped me from speaking. Instead, I let him continue.

"But that's not the most interesting part. The date it was declared off-limits was the same day as your birthday. The exact same day."

"That was the day I was found," I said. "They don't know if it's my actual birthday or not."

"I think someone put Zephyr's egg in the warehouse the same day you were left outside a police station," Minsheng said. "Someone knew one day you'd find each other and bond. It's possible you'd bonded already."

I looked away, all the emotions these words had brought putting a lump in my throat. I still didn't know who my parents were, but to know they meant for me to have Zephyr... That they didn't intend for me to be alone? It made me feel a little more like someone cared about me, someone I'd never met but always longed to.

There were still plenty of questions. I had no idea who the gnome-like man was who had stolen my hairbrush, but I suspected he'd led me to Zephyr deliberately. It was the only explanation that made sense. Minsheng thought it was just a coincidence, however. The glow from the egg had apparently been caused by my presence. No one else would have seen it.

"Oh, crap," Minsheng said. "People."

As he pointed along the beach, I let out a shrill whistle, letting Zephyr know he needed to hurry back to us. We couldn't let him be seen.

While we'd been talking, I'd taken my eyes off Zephyr. I

didn't know where he was anymore and couldn't see his form in the sky above. A knot twisted in my stomach.

Only a few seconds later, relief washed over me as I spotted him flying toward us.

"They've seen him," Minsheng said. "They're pointing at something in the sky."

"That doesn't mean they know it's a dragon. They could think it was an airplane or some kind of bird," I replied.

"Maybe even Superman," he suggested.

If I hadn't been so worried, I'd have laughed. Instead, I beckoned for Zephyr to land. He dived toward me, pulling up at the last moment to stop on his feet and curl up his wings.

He sprayed Minsheng and me with sand, but I didn't care this time. Instead, I ushered him into the car while Minsheng rushed round to the driver's seat

Again Zephyr had to squeeze through the doorframe. As soon as we were all inside, Minsheng floored it, taking us away from the fateful beach and back onto LA's streets.

I leaned into Zephyr, giving him a cuddle. He rested his head against my chest, and I wondered if he was listening to my heartbeat.

"That was too close," I said. "We can't keep going like this. We have to find a better solution, or the agency is going to come after us again."

"I know," Minsheng replied. "We'll work it out. We always do."

I settled back, calming down. I was with the two who mattered to me most, and we were all safe. At least for now.

The End

The adventure continues in Shadow Sworn. *Dragons grow and rules change. Hiding a mythical monster in the heart of LA has never been so hard.*

The story continues with Shadow Sworn, coming April 30, 2021.

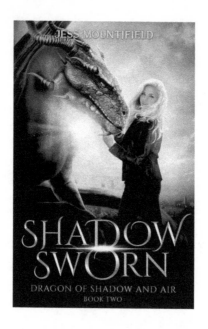

Pre-order now to have your copy delivered as soon as the book is published!

AUTHOR NOTES - JESS MOUNTIFIELD
APRIL 2, 2021

A massive thank you to everyone at LMBPN, especially Michael for taking a chance on Aella and Zephyr. You're all awesome, and I am eternally grateful.

And to everyone at Variant for helping me bring this story to life, especially Jeff, Jen and Kayla. You've been there right from the beginning when Aella and Zephyr were brand new thoughts, right through to letting the world see into their lives for the first time.

Thank you to Ella for the spit and shine and for helping me with my last minute plot issues.

Also huge thank you to my two main writers buddies, David and Bear for the huge series arc plot discussions. I always come away from our chats excited to get writing and with a much clearer picture of who the villains actually are and what they want.

Thank you to all my discord folks who cheered me on, sprinted with me and generally endured as I worked out who everyone was and what I was doing. You're amazing.

To my husband for giving up so much time during a

global pandemic so I could find a quite place in the house and get these words out. I couldn't have managed to write this during 2020 and all the crap it brought with it without your support.

To my tiny humans for occasionally being asleep.

And to God for the continued understanding and for not making mistakes even if I think you should have made elves real.

ABOUT THE AUTHOR

Jess was born in the quaint village of Woodbridge in the UK, has spent some of her childhood in the States and now resides near the beautiful Roman city of Bath. She lives with her husband, Phil, her two tiny humans (one boy and one girl) and her very dapsy cat, Pleaides.

During her still relatively short life Jess has displayed an innate curiosity for learning new things and has therefore studied many subjects, from maths and the sciences, to history and drama. Jess now works full time as a writer and mummy, incorporating many of the subjects she has an interest in within her plots and characters.

When she's not busy with work and keeping her tiny humans alive she can often be found with friends, playing with miniature characters, dice and pieces of paper covered in funny stats and notes about fictional adventures her figures have been on.

You can find out more about the author and her upcoming projects by joining her on facebook, by watching her live D&D streams, or emailing her via books@jessmountifield.co.uk. Jess loves hearing from a happy fan so please do get in touch!

Jess is also opening up her discord for fans to come chat about what she's up to, and see a few sneak peaks of future work. There's also a chance to become one of her beta readers. If you'd like to check that out you can do so <u>here</u>.

Connect with Jess Mountifield

Mailing list sign up
Facebook group.
Discord group
Actual play D&D stream: Twitch or Youtube
Email address: contact me here.

Books by Jess Mountifield

Urban Fantasy

Dragon of Shadow and Air:

Air-Bound

Fantasy

Tales of Ethanar:

Wandering to Belong (Tale 1)

Innocent Hearts (Tale 2 & 3)

For Such a Time as This (Tale 4)

A Fire's Sacrifice (Tale 5)

Winter Series:

The Hope of Winter (Tale 6.05)

The Fire of Winter (Tale 6.1)

Guild of the Eternal Flame:

Wayfarer's Sanctuary

Protector's Secret

Healer's Oath

Other Fantasy:

The Initiate (under Holly Lujah)

Writing with Dawn Chapman:

Jessica's Challenge (#5 in the Puatera Online series)

Dahlia's Shadow (#6 in the Puatera Online series)

Lila's Revenge (#7 in the Puatera Online series)

Sci-Fi:

Fringe Colonies:

Alliance

Haven

Rebellion

Rebirth

Reclamation

Star Trail:

Hunted

Sherdan series:

Sherdan's Prophecy

Sherdan's Legacy

Sherdan's Country

Sherdan's Road (A short story in the anthology 'The End of the Road')

The Slave Who'd Never Been Kissed (A short in the charity anthology 'Imaginings')

New Beginnings

Santa's Little Space Pirate

In the multi-author Adamanta series:

Episode 1 – Adamanta

Episode 3 – Excelsior

Episode 8 – Phoenix

Episode 13 – New Contacts

Episode 17 – Sacrifice

Other:

Clues, Claws and Christmas

Non-Fic:

How to Write Lots, and Get Sh*t Done: the Art of Not Being a Flake

Find purchase links here

Coming soon:

Urban Fantasy:

Dragon of Shadow and Air:

Shadow-Sworn

Dragon-Souled

Earth-Bound

Fantasy

(Tales of Ethanar):

The Pursuit of Winter (#2 in the Winter series, Tale 6.2)

CPSIA information can be obtained
at www.ICGtesting.com
Printed in the USA
BVHW081328231121
622341BV00009B/207

9 781649 716927